ISBN 978-1-64300-272-9 (Paperback)
ISBN 978-1-64300-273-6 (Digital)
Library of Congress Control Number: 2018909956

Covenant Books, Inc.
11661 Hwy 707
Murrells Inlet, SC 29576
www.covenantbooks.com

To my parents: who never told me that my dreams and ideas were unrealistic or unattainable. I always felt as though I could reach for the stars, or at least try as hard as I could.

To Grandpa and Doc: two men in my life that always allowed me to dream big and offered their unique styles of advice along the way. Hard work, humility, and a strong family attitude was always kept squarely in front of me. I was often asked " Would rather live 50 years like a tiger than 100 years like a chicken?"

To my wife: Melanie, who has always listened to even the craziest of ideas and supported whatever dream or outlandish scheme I could come up with next. I would never have been able to do one of the things in my life, let alone all of them, if not for knowing you were always right there beside me.

To Hera: the best dog and friend a person could ask for. Whether I asked you to run in the cold, stand in front of hundreds of school children, comfort the sick, give hugs, peel a banana, or just sit by my side and exist, you did to all with a silly smile. You never paused, said no, or barked. You always hopped right in the car with excitement, as long as we were together. You being you, put the paws in motion for this book to become a reality. Although there is never enough time together in person, you will live on forever in my heart and the pages of this book. Thank you for the times you gave me that big Hera hug. You were, the best.

CHAPTER 1

I am Max. Not Maximus, not Maximilian, and especially not Maxwell. Just plain old Max. I like it like that. Max T. Booker. The "T" does not stand for anything. Just T. My parents liked the name Max but could not decide on whether my middle name should be Terrance or Thomas, each wanting a different name. So they went with just T. I think it suits my personality quite well. I live in town called Carmenville. Carmenville is not a very big town, but it does have its own post office, fuel station, and we are getting our first fast food restaurant at the end of the summer. I live with my mom and dad, my older sister Margaret (Maggie), and my baby brother Benjamin (Benji). I lead a pretty normal nine-year-old life. Well, normal except for my dog, Dash.

I received Dash as a gift at the beginning of this school year, so just about eight months ago. He is still considered a puppy to most; but to me, he is my dog. Not only is Dash my dog, I think of him as my best friend. As long as I am not in school, he is by my side. We go everywhere together, from the store to the barber to my grandparents' house. Yep, two best friends, together forever.

I think it was right around Christmas when I first heard it. We were trudging our way through yet another Midwest snowstorm on our way home when the neighbor's tough dog came charging at us from inside their fence. Usually, Arlo is tied up behind the gate where he can bark all he wants without a chance of him biting us. I guess someone left the gate open or a gust of wind shook it open. Either way, it was open and Arlo was coming out. He was barking and snarling and making all sorts of noise. His teeth were out and slobber was flopping all over his face. I looked at Arlo and started to run. Then I remembered that Dash's legs were not that long so I was

5

worried he would have trouble in the drifted snow. I almost stopped to turn around when I heard it.

"RUN! DON'T STOP! HE WILL EAT US BOTH!"

I was not sure where the voice came from but I grabbed Dash by the collar, scooped him up, and started to run home. Arlo's owner suddenly stormed out from the front door and whistled for Arlo to come back. Like a car screeching to a stop, Arlo threw on the brakes, turned around, and trotted back to his turf. I ran all the way home with Dash in my arms, not because I was afraid of Arlo, but because of the voice I heard. Whose voice was it? Was it that little voice in my head that tells me not to chew gum in school or giggle in church? I never heard it out loud before, but I was certain I heard something. As soon as I got inside, I took my winter clothes off, hung them up, and wiped Dash's paws off, we started to run upstairs to my room.

"Hold on there, bud," my dad said. "I want to hear about the snowball fight. Did your team win?"

I almost forgot where we were coming from! School had been cancelled with all the snow so we went to the park with some of the others from school and had a snowball fight.

"Yeah, it was fine. Nothing too exciting, just your standard snowball fight." I tried to get upstairs to figure out this voice, but dad kept asking questions.

"Was Billy there?"

"Yep," I replied, "we were on the same team. It was Billy, John, and me. We were winning for a while but then a bunch of fifth graders showed up and we were outnumbered. Luckily, it was almost time to head home so I did not get that pummeled with snow. Dash, though, was great. When they would throw the soft ones, he would jump up and catch them with his mouth!"

Dad smiled and told me to kiss Benji on the head and go upstairs to read some of my chapter book. I welcomed being sent to my room as that voice was still in my head. I ran upstairs, gave Dash a treat from the bin on my dresser, and closed the door. He curled up on his bed, as was his normal routine. I opened my book but I could not focus on it so I finally just laid it down. "Whose voice was that?" I said out loud, really to no one.

"Mine." There it was again, the same voice! My skin got all goose bumpy. I looked all around the room, but it was just Dash and me. "I did not want you slowing down. I sure did not want to have to protect you from that Arlo. Did you see how big his teeth were?" I slowly crept down my bed and stared over the edge just in time to see Dash's mouth and lips say, "Whenever you need me, I'll be there."

CHAPTER 2

I stared at Dash as if he was Santa Claus, the Easter Bunny, and the Tooth Fairy all rolled into one four-legged pal. With a very uneasy and shaky voice, I asked, "You . . . you can talk?"

"Yep!" Dash replied. "All dogs can talk. We do it all the time. I am not the special one. You are."

I had no idea what to say. My puppy, my best friend, my *dog* was talking to me! As I stared at him, he rolled over on his back, waiting for me to rub his belly.

Maggie came bursting through my door. "Keep that fleabag quiet! I am trying to talk to Grace on the phone about our algebra homework! If you can't keep him quiet, I will have to call Mom at work and tell her he is bothering me." And as quickly and ferociously as she came in, she was gone.

"I don't care for her much," Dash said in a whisper. "She is just mean."

"Don't mind her, she is easy to deal with. We do have to stay quiet though. I don't want her calling Mom at work."

Our house is different than most. My mom goes to work and my dad stays home with Benji during the day, doing house chores and such. They both had a job when I was little but once Benji was born, Dad quit his job as a zookeeper and Mom kept working as a journalist. I hate it when Maggie calls Mom at work to rat me out. It just makes Mom mad at me, mad at Dash, and most of all, mad at Dad. It's just easier to try to get along with everyone.

I heard the garage door opening and quickly knew Mom was home. I ran downstairs to greet her. When she gets home, we all meet in the kitchen to tell each other all about our days. Maggie goes first, then me, and then Benji gets his attention. Dad usually has his newest supper invention ready to try, and we sit down to eat. Every night, it's the same thing. We eat as a family, talk about our day, and then, depending on whose turn it is on the big board, they have to do the dishes.

"Max," Mom chirped, "how was your day off? Are you in there?" I quickly shook my head and smiled. "Daydreaming again, huh?" she asked.

"It was great," I replied. I was having a hard time focusing on what everyone was saying. I just really wanted to go back upstairs and talk to Dash. I hurried through supper. Luckily, it was Maggie's turn to do the dishes. As soon as I was excused, I bounded up the stairs to my room. Dash, who was right behind me, immediately curled up on his bed and drifted off to sleep. He was asleep before I could ask him anything. I did not dare wake him up as my grandfather always told me to let sleeping dogs lie. He woke up only once to go out and was back asleep before I felt comfortable opening up a discussion.

Over the months since—well, five to be exact—Dash answered all of my questions. All dogs can talk, understand, and reply to each other about what humans say. No matter what the language, a dog can understand it. The problem is, only a handful of humans can communicate with dogs. When a dog barks, they are actually speaking. So what I hear as Dash talking, everyone else I know just hears "*Woof!*" My ability to communicate is not just limited to Dash. I can talk to and understand all the dogs in the neighborhood.

In the beginning, Dash told me to play along and act like I could not understand what was being said. We would go to the dog park with my parents and it was hard not to laugh out loud or give my two cents into their conversations. Now that school is letting out soon for summer, we will be outside all day and visit Dash's friends more often. His best dog friends are Annie, Hera, and Waldo. Annie and Hera live with the Odells, our next-door neighbors. Doc Odell and his wife do not have any children so Annie and Hera fit into that role nicely. Annie is small but has a lot of energy and spunk. Hera is tall but dainty. She prances around like a queen. When they start chasing each other though, watch out! It is like a racetrack! Waldo lives across the street with Billy and his dad. Billy's mom died from cancer a couple years ago before they moved to Carmenville. Billy and I are friends. Next to Dash, he is my best friend. We have always been in the same classroom together. Waldo is Dash's best buddy. They are both about the same age, just like Billy and me. Whenever the four of us go out on walks or to explore the forest and streams near the park, we are all together. Best friends forever!

CHAPTER 3

"**W**ake up, Max! It's finally here. Today is the last day of school. At noon, you will be out for the summer and we can be together all the time!" I rolled over just in time to get a lick to the face. Every morning at seven o'clock, Dash would wake me up the same way. A bellowing "Wake up, Max!" followed by a wet lick. I quickly pulled back the covers, hopped out of bed, ran past Maggie into the bathroom, and got ready.

Maggie started to pound on the door just as I was finishing brushing my teeth. "You know I have to get to school early today, Max. Grace and I have to study for our literature final," she scolded me as I walked out of the bathroom. She slammed the door as she went in.

"I would not ever want to be in high school," commented Dash as I picked out my favorite shirt and shorts. "She seems to always be in a hurry or something. I don't quite understand her sometimes."

"Me neither, Dash. Me neither," I replied on my way downstairs for breakfast.

As I made my way into the kitchen, Dad already poured my chocolate cereal with lots of milk. I like lots of milk because when I am done, Dash gets to lick the rest out of the bowl. Well, only if Mom is not around. I asked Dad if Mom had left yet. He told me she had but she was covering the last day of school for the paper so she would meet me at school to pick up my report card. I almost forgot about that. Report card day was the last thing standing in my way before summer vacation. I only had four more hours of Mr. Mathews, my lousy fourth grade teacher. I cannot imagine a more miserable person on planet Earth. He never smiled and was mean, nasty, and had a very unique smell about him. (I was told to try to never say anything bad about anyone. Mr. Mathews never did smile, and he was mean, nasty. But the smell . . . well, that's about as nice as I can make it.) I said good-bye to Dash. He said good luck. Then I was off across the street to get Billy. We made our way to school, half jogging and half hopping the whole way. We had big plans this summer. As soon-to-be fifth graders, we were going to be allowed to go to the pool alone, walk down to the bowling alley during the day, and maybe even ride our bikes further down the trails than last year.

As we entered room 12, the bell rang. Mr. Mathews took attendance and started instructing us on how he wanted an orderly line to hand in our textbooks. Every other class in the school had done this days ago while we were still reading silently and figuring out math problems. At eleven thirty, the bell rang and our parents came in. My mom and Billy's dad came together. Billy's dad opened his report card up, cracked a small smile, and motioned for Billy to come up. Billy's dad thanked Mr. Mathews and whispered into

Billy's ear. The expression on Billy's face looked as if his dad told him they were having liver for supper! Billy shrugged, stuck his hand out for Mr. Mathews to shake, and thanked him for the wonderful school year. I was shocked, but I had bigger things to worry about. My astronomy science project was not stellar and my spelling tests were less than perfect so I was a little nervous when my mom opened up my report card. There was no smile on her face. She gave me the "Come here, Max" look, and I knew things were not good. However, I had a great idea. As soon as I got to the front of the room, I stuck my hand out for Mr. Mathews to shake and thanked him for the wonderful school year. My Mom smiled from ear to ear! Mr. Mathews was shocked more than anyone. On our way out of the school, Mom commented that although my final grades were not what my parents had hoped for, I had obviously matured that year. It worked! One brief handshake would keep me from being inside all summer.

As soon as we were home, Billy and Waldo were over, and we scrambled over the fence into the Odell's yard for all four dogs to play.

"Listen, Annie," Hera said, "the rest of us have been talking, and we are sick and tired of you biting our ankles all the time. It is way too warm out here to be running around chasing each other."

I smirked, knowing how much Dash hated to be bitten by little Annie. Dash spoke up and agreed. "Yeah, it is too hot and annoying to be bitten at all. Please stop it!"

Annie ignored both requests and ran after Waldo so as to not bother the two that had just spoken up. I yelled Annie's name, telling her to stop it. She ran over to me and looked up. "Why?" she barked.

"Because they asked so nicely," I replied. The look on her face was amazing as her ears flopped out like Dumbo.

Billy laughed and said, "It is like she understands you, Max. Look at her!"

I winked at Billy and said, "I speak dog."

Dash looked at the others and said, "Yep, Max understands us all. We have been communicating since just before Christmas." The three other dogs did not know what to say.

"Why didn't you tell us, Dash?" whimpered Annie.

"You have been keeping that a secret from us?" howled Waldo.

Hera just laid in the sun in silence. She was too upset to even speak. Just then, Billy chased Waldo through the yard, and the others joined in. It was just Dash and I left on the patio.

"They were going to find out sometime," said Dash. "I figured the start of the summer would be as fine of a time as any. I understand they may be upset, but I had to keep it from them. Not everyone can adjust to knowing a human can understand us." I could tell Dash felt bad about not being truthful and honest with his friends over the past few months, but I figured he knew what was best.

Soon enough, Hera galloped over to us, nosed Dash to play, and looked at me. "I always knew you were special," she said very matter-of-factly. "I hope you understand what a fabulous gift you have." With that, she and Dash ran off after the other two.

Billy hopped over the fence and grabbed the whiffle ball set. As he tossed the bat and ball back over the fence, he stood on the top rail and declared, "This is our summer."

"It sure is," howled the four dogs in unison. "Our summer!"

CHAPTER 4

Even though it was summer, Dash still woke me up the same way every day. "Wake up, Max!" I was reminded every morning at seven o'clock that the new day had arrived. If I attempted to roll over, I would get another lick. If I managed to ignore the first two, Dash would jump up on my bed and sit right on my chest. Very rarely did I ignore the second lick. With Maggie out of school too, I had to try to keep Dash as quiet as I could while she was sleeping. Some days she would not get up until almost noon so those days we spent most of the morning outside. My daily routine consisted of breakfast with Mom, Dad, and Benji; taking Dash for his morning walk; and then meeting up with Billy and Waldo. The mornings usually had us riding bicycles and exploring the wooded area at the back of our yard and then lunch. Billy always had lunch at our house during the summer. His dad worked during the day so we spent all day together until supper. The afternoons were wide open, from swimming at the pool to reading at the library and almost everything in between. Since school had only been out about a week, the summer looked as though it was a blank canvas.

On my way back from walking Dash, we began to talk about what to do today.

"How about we all head down the bicycle path?" asked Dash. "I know Waldo and I can outrun Billy and you on your bicycles. You have the advantage, but we are still faster," he boasted. "Much faster."

I felt challenged by my best friend and really wanted to prove him wrong. I was a little worried about how far we could go on the path alone so early in the summer. If we traveled too far, our dads might tell us no more exploring down the path for the rest of the summer. But if we did not go far enough, Dash and Waldo would almost definitely win as they were better in the short runs. As Billy rode up the driveway, I figured I would see what he thought of the challenge.

"Sure," said Billy, "Let's head down to the old Owl Oak. We have been there tons of times before, and we can look to see if there are any birds' nests from the spring!"

Dash and Waldo both smirked, commenting to each other that they had us beat. "Why not head down the trail a bit further, Billy? We always stop at the Owl Oak. Maybe there's something better down the trail," I suggested.

The reply from Billy came swift and firm. "Nope, I am riding only as far as the Owl Oak." He turned his bicycle around and headed toward the trailhead. I could tell that he was upset at the thought of going further.

Dash and Waldo stayed by our sides while we were still in town. "As soon as we are in the clearing, the race starts," yelled Dash.

"First team to the Owl Oak is declared the winner," howled Waldo. "Triumph will be ours." Billy looked back and commented on how both dogs were loud today.

"Yeah, must be the warmer weather," I said. "It must be something."

I tried to conserve some energy for the trail but did not want to fall too far behind either. Dash did look back constantly to make sure I was within barking distance. I knew he was safe with Waldo up front. They had both been on this trail in early spring, and knew where to go. When Billy and I made the turn into the clearing, I was surprised to see both Dash and Waldo basking in the sun on the path.

"We are just soaking up the sun before our fun begins," Dash howled. "To make it a fair race, we will not start until both bicycles have crossed the dirt path." I thought it was very fair of them to give us an even chance.

As soon as our tires crossed though, I heard Waldo yell, "Go!"

And we were all off. Billy and I pedaled as fast as we could. Billy was having trouble just keeping up with me. He had no idea why I was pedaling so hard so he kept asking, "Why are you going so fast?" The dogs were well ahead of us, but I could still see them. After a few moments though, they were out of sight. I slowed down, knowing that we had lost. We had lost a race that my best friend did not even know we were in. "Where are the dogs?" asked Billy. "Where did they go? They better not be lost," he said, his voice cracking a little bit.

"They know the path, Billy, don't worry about it. I'm sure they ran out to the Owl Oak and stopped around there somewhere," I tried to reassure him. How do you tell someone you know something without telling him how you know? It was obvious Billy was concerned about where his dog was.

After a silent fifteen-minute ride, we arrived at the Owl Oak. I was so excited to see the crown of the Owl Oak just over the crest of the last rolling hill. As we coasted down the hill, my eyes darted back and forth across the path and landscape to see if I could spot the dogs. Nothing. I looked back and saw Billy almost crying.

"Why did we have to ride so fast?" he asked. "The faster we went, the faster the dogs ran. It was like you were in a race or something. Now the dogs are lost and I'm tired."

I felt horrible. Both Dash and Waldo were still puppies, just under a year old. I was almost ten. I knew better than to be talked into a race that I knew we were going to lose and where something bad may happen. I had nothing to say to Billy. He was right. "Don't worry, Bill," I said. "They will be around somewhere." I only wished I was convinced in what I had just said. The look on his face was how we both felt.

We rested our bicycles against the Owl Oak. Neither one of us knew what to do. We screamed their names as loud as we could. No response. We walked down the path up to the top of the next hill and squinted to see if we could see any sign of them. Nothing.

"I'm scared Max," said Billy. As I looked over at him, I saw a look on his face that I told myself I never wanted to see again.

"We will find them, Billy, trust me. Together forever." As we both searched the ground for any clue they were there, I glanced at my watch. It was eleven thirty. We had to be at the table when both hands were on the twelve. "After lunch, we will come straight back and keep up the search," I said. "Maybe by then they will have figured out our scent and made their way here."

I really had no idea where they were or even if we would find them. I was starting to lose hope. We pedaled our bicycles back to my house. It was a long ride. What took no time at all on the way out seemed to take double going home.

"What are we going to tell your dad?" Billy asked.

"I was thinking the same thing. If we tell him we lost the dogs, both our dads are going to make us keep them on leashes," I said. "Let's just tell them they are in your yard." I looked over and saw that Billy was not real excited about that answer.

"I don't like to lie, especially when we probably need your dad's help," he said. "But in this case, it will at least get us through lunch."

As we reached the once start line, we pedaled hard to get home. "The faster we get home, the faster we are done with lunch, the faster we are back out looking for them," I said.

"Agreed," replied Billy. "Snap, snap, snap."

We turned up my driveway and parked out bicycles next to the garage. My dad came out on the back porch and smiled.

"How was the ride, gents?" he asked. "Any good looking owls' nests out there?"

I did not know how to answer. I really wanted to tell him both Dash and Waldo were missing. I wanted his help finding them. I wanted to tell him to call the police, the fire department, someone to find my dog. Just as I was about to break down and cry right there on the porch, Maggie opened up the door, and out came Dash and Waldo running.

"Howdy, boys!" yelped Dash.

"What took you so long?" bellowed Waldo.

"There you are!" exclaimed Billy, almost in tears.

"They came back about forty-five minutes ago," said Dad. "I figured you two were going too fast for them so they turned around and came home. These are two smart pups if I have ever seen them. Let's have some lunch."

We all went inside for sandwiches and lemonade. After lunch when we were all over in the Odell's yard playing and chasing each other, I asked Dash, "What happened? Where did you two go? Why didn't you stop at the Owl Oak?"

"We ran and ran and ran. Soon we lost sight of you and Billy. I thought we ran too far so we cut across the open field and came home. I was worried and scared when we lost you, but I knew how to get back home. We never made it to the old Owl Oak," Dash said calmly. "We both knew Billy and you would just come home."

"We were scared, Dash," I told him. "We were afraid we lost you both."

"So were we, Max," replied Dash. "Let's never race again. Together is the best way to be!" As he ran off after Annie, he turned his head and said, "Congratulations on the victory!"

I smiled and took running off after Hera and Waldo. The rest of our day was spent in the safe confines of the Odell's yard, tossing a Frisbee and playing catch.

CHAPTER 5

The next couple of weeks came and went wonderfully with Billy, Waldo, Dash, and me spending as much time as we could together. Our parents had a meeting with us about a week after school let out, telling us that we could spend the night at each other's houses every night, unless we were told specifically that we would not be able to. That glorious tidbit of news laid the foundation for what was a going to be the best summer ever. The first half would live up to those expectations.

With the Fourth of July shining on the horizon like the sun at sunrise, Billy and I knew that we would have to really start planning for something big and important. Maybe the most important event of a soon to be ten-year-old's summer. The Fourth of July bicycle parade! Every summer during Carmenville's Fourth of July parade, all the children decorate their bikes, scooters, buggies, and big wheels with a wide selection of bows, streamers, balloons, and posters. The bigger the better. The more patriotic and brilliant, the better the chance of winning one of the five prizes. Four of the prizes were awarded based on what was used to decorate the entries: best use of streamers, best use of balloons, best use of handmade crafts, and loudest noisemakers. Everyone who entered knew that if you won one of these categories, you were out of the running for the biggest, the best, and the one that gave you 365 days of bragging rights—the most patriotic!

With only two weeks left until the big day, Billy and I went straight into planning mode during breakfast. With Maggie still in bed, we were able to talk freely about our ideas without the threat of her stealing what we came up with. I knew my dad could be trusted not to tell anyone, and with Dash and Waldo both scouring the floor for the random kibble, we were safe. Billy kept wanting to wrap the handlebars of our bikes with streamers and put balloons on the handgrips, which was what everyone else was doing. I wanted new ideas. I wanted us to stand out. We needed stunning. What we needed was help brainstorming. When we both finished our toast and rinsed off our plates and cups, we were out into the backyard in a flash. When there was deep thinking to be done, we each had our own lawn chair, and the dogs would chase each other or relax in the shade of the big maple tree.

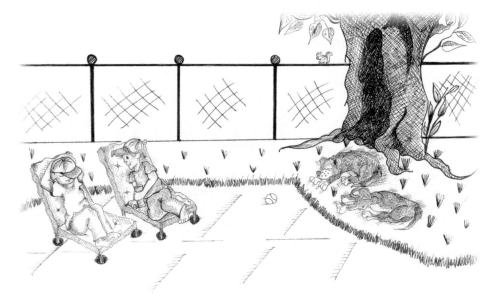

As Billy started to make a list of what we needed for supplies, Dash barked out, "A human-and-canine-powered float! If we can come up with something like a stage that can be pulled, then there can be a play put on *during* the parade!"

"That's perfect!" I yelled, startling Billy so much that he dropped his pencil.

"What?" Billy squawked. "I have no idea what you just said. How about including your partner in on the great idea."

I did not know how to answer him because the float idea was not mine to begin with. Dash and Waldo knew just what to do so they started running toward the maple tree and barking wildly, making it seem like they saw a squirrel. As Dash and Waldo barked and howled at the imaginary critter, I translated Dash's parade idea for Billy who was now on the edge of his seat with anticipation.

"We figure out a way to have one person in front pulling on a rope that is connected to a makeshift stage. The rope can be hooked on to a bicycle. Next to the person on the bicycle is a dog, making it look like the dog and person in front are 'pulling' the float," I told Billy. "Behind the bicycle is a piece of wood on a few skateboards that will be decorated to make it look like a stage."

"And on the stage," howled Waldo, getting more and more squeakier with every word, "is a scene depicting America's history!"

Billy dropped his pencil in the grass and smiled ear to ear. "Max, that's the best idea you have ever come up with! Let's start planning and building immediately. Ten days may not be enough to bring this idea together," Billy excitedly said with spit flying out of his mouth. "How did you ever come up with such a brilliant idea?" he asked in delight and awe.

I shrugged my shoulders, feeling a little bit guilty for having to tell him a nontruth, and said, "It came to me a little earlier today. Yeah, it came to me about seven this morning when Dash woke me up." I looked over to Dash and Waldo just in time to see them look back at us on the patio, both of them wagging their tails with delight knowing that the next ten days were going to be an adventure like none other so far.

CHAPTER 6

As that Monday came and went, Billy and I talked all day about ideas. When an idea for a scene of American history was really bad, I would get a loud "Nope!" from Dash and Waldo. If the idea was really bad, all four would be howling and yelping. Just before supper, however, the yard erupted with so many barks that even I had to turn around to see what was going on. I immediately thought this might be the worst idea yet, but to my surprise, Dash and Waldo were bounding across the yard, barking as loud as they could. When they were close enough for me to hear what they were saying, I was delighted to hear a chorus of "Yes, yes, yes, yes, yes! That's it!" Waldo screamed.

"That is the winning idea!" howled Dash.

Billy turned to the yard and said, "They must have just heard or seen something they were scared of."

As I had been lost in my own train of thought, I asked Billy, "What was your last idea? That one seemed like the best so far."

"George Washington," he quietly said, trying to bring the noise level back down from a college roar. "George Washington crossing the Pottowatomie River."

"Potomac River," both Dash and I said in unison. "Potomac."

With that, the next ten days of our summer were planned out. Billy spent that night at home with his dad because he had an early dentist appointment the next morning. I thought that was perfect as I wanted to talk to Dash about how he thought this float idea was going to work.

"When we go to other parades down Main Street," Dash said, "there are always floats. The adults make these big floats with flowers, bows, and more flowers. Then behind are the kids with their bicycles.

I think we need to step it up, you know, become more adult." Dash went on, "How can we participate in the parade if we are not really participating in the parade?" Dash sometimes talked in sentences I did not understand. This was one of those times. I nodded my head like I understood, but Dash was able to see I still had some questions. "We watched videos of the Thanksgiving Day parades, and they all have floats. Huge ones. And monster balloons. Then we watch the after Christmas football day parade, and they have floats, huge ones with flowers. What we lack in material and know-how we will make up in desire and spunk!"

We sat up talking until Mom came in to gently remind us to go to sleep, drawing and sketching out how the best float in the parade would come to be. Dash and I were up with the sun. Even before breakfast was cooked, I was out in the garage, taking inventory of what materials we had. When Dad opened up the screen door to tell me breakfast was ready, I startled him by popping my head out from underneath the staircase, asking, "What are we having today?"

"Toast, bacon, jam, and chocolate milk," he said, smiling at my surprise location.

"Did you remember to save the bacon fat for Dash?" I inquired, just like every other time he made bacon.

"Of course!" Dad said with a little bit of a laugh. "I only wish you cared about your chores as much as Dash's extra food snacks. Remember, today is weed-pulling day in the front garden and lawn. And you *have* to do it today since you talked your way out of it last week and the week before that. Your mother is going to be really mad at the two of us if her garden is not cleaned up and cleared of dandelions."

My heart sank. Today was day one of our float build. It seemed like we were going to be dead in the water before we even started. I trudged inside and plopped down on my chair. I took my knife and made a half-hearted swipe at smearing raspberry jam on my toast. I just knew that Billy was going to be so disappointed that we were not going to get our float made. I kept going through the days until the parade in my head, knowing that if we lost just *one* build day, there was no way that we could pull this idea off. I must have looked horribly sullen because as I was drinking my milk, a cold wet nose nudged my sun-drenched calf.

"*Psst*! Hey, look down here," came a familiar but curious voice. "*Psst!* Look down here!" I pushed my chair back just a little, only to see little Annie dog in our kitchen! "Dash came out and said that you might have some problems with weeds. I am the best dirt digger in the county. You point me in the right direction, I will have the whole garden tore up before you know it."

I stared down at Annie just a few seconds too long because here came Maggie, giving orders to everyone and everything in sight. "Who keeps getting these dogs excited to the point that they will not be quiet?" questioned Maggie about ten times as loud as either Dash or Annie barked. "Where is that mangy mongrel? He better not eat any of my share of the bacon!" she bellowed.

I backed away from the table just enough for Maggie to see that it was not Dash I was petting and hiding under the table, but Annie, the Odell's little brown dog. "As if one four-legged vermin was not enough!" screamed Maggie down the stairs to my dad who was doing laundry. "But now he thinks he can bring the whole neighborhood of dogs in for breakfast? When will this calamity end?" Maggie must have noticed that I wrinkled my nose with "calamity," like I do when someone says something I do not understand, because she very calmly and patiently said, "Calamity, an event causing great and often sudden damage or distress, a disaster. Like Calamity Jane."

I did not know who this Jane person was and I really did not want to meet another one of Maggie's friends. I took the opportunity of Dad being downstairs to grab the last couple of pieces of bacon off the lazy Susan, rinse my plate and glass off, and lunged out the back door, quickly being followed by Annie who, from the sounds of it, gave Maggie her special "ankle nip" just prior to leaving.

"I don't think she will be sending me a Christmas card this year," exclaimed Annie. With that, we were off to clear some weeds.

CHAPTER 7

When I walked out to the front garden, Dash was already basking in the early morning sun. Next to him lay Hera, all stretched out like Superman when he flies. Neither one of them seemed to pay any attention to either Annie or me. As I glanced over to see if Billy was back from the dentist, I saw Waldo springing up and down behind the gate, barking wildly. I could not hear what he was saying so I asked Dash.

"Aw, he's just blathering on and on about how he is the best weed popper in the county. We all know there is no one better than Annie. She has an unlimited power reserve and the attention span of a gnat so she is easily amused by every weed!" exclaimed Dash. "If you go let him out of Billy's yard, that is just opening this situation up for disaster."

I intently looked at Dash and said, "When did I ever walk away from a good disaster?" Half joking and half knowing things never seem to work out as planned. Before I could even finish my sentence, I was on the curb, looking both ways before I crossed the street to bring Waldo over for the morning's digging extravaganza.

After everyone had said hello and made sure they were familiar with each other (you know, that thing dogs do with each other to say hello—the butt sniffing!), I told everyone not only the goal, but the "anti goal." "This is my mom's prize-winning flower garden. The mayor would hand out ribbons and prizes in the parade and also to the home with the best flower garden and vegetables. My mom won every year for the past seven years! I was supposed to pull weeds weekly but . . . well, *umm*, I haven't. My dad says that if I want to be able to continue on with the float-building project, I have to get the entire garden weed free as well as the front lawn," I said.

"We will have this whole garden turned over in no time," Annie barked as she lunged her tiny little paws into the soft morning soil. "No time at all!"

"STOP!" I screamed at the top of my lungs. "Stop! There are other rules that we have to stick to. There are not only flowers on top of the soil, but there are bulbs beneath the soil, which we also can't disturb. If we dig too deep or go too fast, the tulip bulbs will be disturbed, and next spring will be a disaster. We need to go slow."

I looked down the line of four-legged gardeners and everyone's tail was wagging in all directions, except for Dash. Annie's tail was going round and round like a Danish windmill. Waldo's was thumping up and down so hard on the grass that little tufts of green grass were sputtering up around him. Hera's tail went left to right, having cleaned a tail-sized swath on the concrete walk. Then there was Dash. Dash was lying down, resting his head and long snout on his front paws.

"This, Max, is a bad idea. We know nothing about digging safely and neatly. Dogs do not dig holes cleanly. Dogs dig holes to hide bones, sniff out things they have hidden, find lovely things to roll around in, or even holes to sit in when it's hot outside. Giving the go ahead for this crew to help dig out weeds in Mom's prized garden is . . . well, it's just plain—" Dash said, stopping quickly midsentence.

As I took my gaze off him up to the sky and back down to him, I saw his tail droop. He was staring intently at something to my right. As I started to look down, I heard Waldo say, "You probably don't want to look down just yet."

With that, I looked straight down only to see Annie's front paws covered in mud, little pieces and bits of dirt stuck to her little pink nose, and a large sunflower head hanging from her jaws. She must have seen the look for horror on my face because she gently put it at my feet and said, "I had a rough start. Let's put this behind us and move on!" I had to laugh at not only her gentle way of being, but also that Dash was able to predict this scenario so perfectly before it even started.

After a quick lesson on weeds versus flowers and a heated discussion on whether or not dandelions were flowers or not, my weed-pulling crew were on their way. "Dash," I said loud enough so that the whole team could hear, "you were right about Annie! Look at her go!" Annie had a system in place that worked wonderfully for her little body. She would put her nose right in front of the weed in question, stick her butt up in the air like she was playing or ready to pounce, and then let her little paws and nails to the rest. Dirt flew in every direction, but in a few seconds there were no weeds! Although her style was very effective in the getting the weeds out, it was rather ineffective in the leaving no hole behind part. Annie's digging required me to come behind and fill all of her holes back in. "A small price to pay, Annie girl," I told her. "A small price to pay for such enthusiasm."

I left Annie to work on her area while I went down to see what Waldo and Hera were up to. Waldo and Hera are older than Annie and Dash by a few years at least. They were usually talking to each other when the group was near each other, comparing stories about life and things that they had heard humans say. Hera was very stately. Dash said that she was the queen of the group.

"I have no problem being the queen," Hera once said, "as long as I am not considered the court jester."

"That sounds like a perfect role for me," exclaimed Annie.

"I do not think you are going to get much of an argument there," Dash said in passing. Waldo never said much but when he did, everyone around him listened. Dash was a leader of sorts. The youngest by years, Dash had a certain maturity about him. He was a solid dog, not too tall to be considered lanky and not too short to run fast. "I listen to everything that I can hear from humankind and learn," he would often tell new dogs at the dog park. Today was no different. Hera and Waldo were both sitting down and staring at a small hole Waldo had dug. It was wider than Annie's but not very deep. I had a hard time hearing what they were saying to each other as they were speaking very softly.

"Secrets, secrets, they're no fun. Secrets, secrets, hurt someone," I bellowed out, staring directly at them to see if what they were saying fit into that category.

"Secrets? Who, us? No. Never. Nope," denied Hera. "We would never keep anything from you."

As Hera was getting the last of that sentence out, Waldo blurted out, "We think there is a big pile of horse compost underneath there and I want to roll around in it!" It was then that I remembered a few weeks back, I helped my mom put mushroom compost in the front garden. It was stinky! Just as Waldo was making his way into the garden to roll in the stink, I was able to grab him and keep him clean. "Please! Just one roll, Max, please!" begged Waldo. "I promise I will be your best friend for life. I will dig the rest of the weeds up myself. I . . . I . . . I!" he continued, running out of things a dog can promise a human.

As he was trying to think of other things to say, Dash calmly reminded us all of today's ultimate goal, which was to work on the float. "We need to get the weeds out and the garden leveled so when Billy gets home, we can start the parade float," Dash said. "Let's keep our noses down and our paws a-movin'."

With that, my canine work crew was back on task. Over the next few hours or so, we managed to get all of the weeds out of the flower garden without any major losses. There were a few marigold heads torn off here and there. There were even rose petals shaken off, thorns and all. I looked around and saw that we had completed the job. The morning was just about over as I was leveling out the dirt and making sure I had everything put back and cleaned up. My crew all were given a congratulatory pig ears to chew on in the shade as a thank you for all of their hard work.

Just as we were all finished, I heard Waldo howl, "Billy's home!"

CHAPTER 8

I quickly looked up to see Billy and his dad getting out of the car. I waved at him and quickly ran over to the curb of the street, making sure to look both ways before I crossed and that my gardening crew were all across safely.

"How was the dentist?" I asked Billy. He did not give me his normal smile or laugh, which made me wonder what had happened.

"Billy does not look just right," Waldo noted. "He looks sad for some reason. I wonder if he had too many cavities or if he was told that he had to floss more."

"I am glad that we do not have to go to the dentist's office," Annie whined in her high-pitched squeal. "From what I have heard, it's not much fun."

"It is not too bad," I replied out loud, getting a very odd look from Billy's dad.

"Did you say something?" he asked. "It sounded like you answered a question but no one asked one, unless you are replying to Annie's bark!"

"Nope, just thinking out loud," I quickly said. "Just thinking out loud." I immediately turned around to look at Billy. That was the closest I have ever been to being caught talking to the dogs. If he thought it was weird that I answered a dog's bark, imagine what he would think if he knew that I was actually talking to them? As Billy's Dad walked up the driveway and into the house, I looked at Billy, still standing next to the car door. "Too many cavities? Not enough flossing? Was the pirate's chest prize box empty?" I asked in rapid sequence. "What's the story?"

Billy answered with only one word. A word that kids have hated since the beginning of time. A word that would make even the strongest and toughest bully break down. This one word meant so many things. No gum. No popcorn. No eating apples one chomp at a time. No eating corn straight off the cob. No more smiling.

"Braces," he muttered.

My heart sank for him. He would be the first of my close friends that was told he needed them. Sure, his teeth were a bit crooked and he had a bit of an overbite, but braces? "Are they sure? Is there anything else that can be done?" I asked.

"They are positive," Billy replied. "I will most likely need them on for a couple of years. The special dentist, an orthodontist, measured my teeth and took imprints of them all. The only good news I got today is that I don't have to get them put on until school starts back up in September."

As Billy was talking, I watched as his loyal and always present buddy, Waldo, slowly walked over to him. Waldo sat down right next to Billy and used his snout to move Billy's hand over to pet his head. "Don't worry, buddy," Waldo tried to comfort Billy. "It is not going to be the worst thing in your life. We will all be right here for you, especially me. If I can figure out a way to go into the dentist's office with you, I will." Waldo whimpered in a way that made every word louder and louder.

"We all will be right there for you, Billy," howled Hera and Annie in exact precise unison. If only he could understand what the dogs were saying to him. By this point, all everyone else in the area heard was four dogs howling. "Right there until the end!" was the chant that Dash came up with.

"Right there until the end!" I exclaimed, showing our four legged friends just how much I loved being able to hear them and translate into human words. This made Billy smile, seeing that I was talking just as the dogs were barking. "We are friends for life, Billy," I told him. "Plus, we have the rest of the summer to conquer. Not to mention, we have the Fourth of July parade to work on and win before we even think about going back to school."

"Our float!" exclaimed Billy. "I was so caught up in the dentist and what the orthodontist was telling me that I forgot about our float! Let's go grab some lunch and then knuckle down and start on the construction."

As the two of us raced up the driveway, closely followed by our gang of canines, I could not help but think how life was changing. We were growing up. We were getting older. We were able to go farther on our bicycles without an adult. We were able to walk to the ice cream stand alone. Now Billy was getting braces. I wanted everything to slow down and stay the same. Just as I was starting to feel really sad, a cold wet nose nudged my hand.

"Can you smuggle me out a piece of bacon?" asked Dash. "Extra crispy please."

I looked down to see my best friend sitting with his tail wagging side to side, brushing off the dust and dirt on the concrete driveway. "Only if you promise to never change, Dash."

"Deal," barked Dash. "Deal."

CHAPTER 9

As we finished up lunch, Billy's dad asked up if we had any ideas how we were going to decorate our bikes for the parade. "Now that you two are getting older, the expectations are going to be higher. I think you both have a great chance at winning," he said. "With the Martins having moved this past winter, you two have the most experience in the parade. I think you both will do great!"

"We have been kicking an idea around that will floor everyone, including you and Max's parents," said Billy. "It's amazing. We have to start working on it this afternoon or there might not be enough time before the parade."

"The parade is just over ten days away," Billy's dad exclaimed. "If you start decorating your bikes now, you won't be able to ride them until the Fourth. You don't want to put yourselves on your feet for that long and not be able to ride, do you?" We could tell that he was getting very curious. "What do you two have up your sleeves? I can tell by the look on Max's face that this is a big one. A blue-ribbon idea?"

"Well, yes," replied Billy. "Yes and no, all at once. It is a really good idea that is going to take a lot of hard work and planning. But today is the first day of the build."

"The build?!" exclaimed Billy's dad. "Build? What are you two planning other than bicycle decorating? It is usually streamers, ribbons, and baseball cards in the spokes to make noise. I am not sure anyone has ever *built* anything as an entry before," he said as his voice came up at the end to punctuate the question. "A build?"

"Yup, a build," Billy said proudly. "A build."

"Well, I sure don't want to be the one to stand in front of greatness, but I think we need to sit down with Max's dad and go over some ground rules for this project. Safety first. There can be no ignoring safe work shop practices. No *if*, *ands*, or *buts* about it. Let me call over and see if your dad will come over and talk, Max," Billy's dad said. We could hear him talking on the phone, laughing at times and waving his arms wildly in the other room.

"I wish I knew what he was saying to your dad," Billy said as he paced back and forth in the kitchen.

As soon as Billy had gotten that statement out of his mouth, I saw Dash slowly crawl on the floor over to a patch of sunlight streaming through the front room windows just a few feet past the kitchen wall. "I am not sure what these two are up to, Dave, but they are up to something. They are talking about building something for the Fourth parade. Yeah, I know. That's what I said. *Uh-huh!* Yeah, safety first. Okay, I'll see you in a couple of minutes," Dash quietly barked out for me to translate.

I knew there was not enough time for me to tell Billy so I just told him what I thought they were saying, guessing what most dads might say. "Max, your dad is on his way over so we can go over some ground rules. I know how much the parade means to you both, but we can't have you getting hurt for a parade," he told us. Immediately following his statement, the bell rang and the back door opened.

"Mike, it's nice to see you. We need to make more time and get together with these knuckleheads more often," my dad said to Billy's dad.

"I know, Dave. We live just across the street and hardly see each other. But at least our boys are close. They remind me of us when we were younger!" Bill's dad said to mine. "And it sounds like they are carrying on the tradition of adventure-filled summers. I am not sure what they have going on or if they are going to be willing to share their ideas with us. I'm fine with the secrecy as long as the rules of working with tools are followed and none of their chores are neglected."

"I agree a hundred percent, Mike," my dad stated. "Let's just lay them out and see how well our boys listen and follow. This is going to be very simple, guys. Both of you have to still do all of your housework and chores. You have to pay attention and do whatever the parents say needs to be done without any talking back. There is to be zero use of power tools unless one of us is standing right there. And, most of all—"

"If you think it's unsafe, it probably is!" Billy's dad, Mr. Rhu, interrupted. "I don't want to see anything happen to either of you. I have no problem with having fun but if it ends with an injury, it just was not worth it."

I looked over to see a huge smile on Billy's face, something I had not seen all morning up until this point. My dad stuck his hand out to shake, and the four of us all shook hands in agreement. We would be allowed to work on our secret parade project alone until we needed help with the big parts, then we would ask for help. As we shook hands, I asked both dads to shake on secrecy that they would not dare tell anyone our idea. Upon the handshake, Billy and I both lowered our voices to a whisper. We talked about our plan and how the build needed to proceed. How we wanted to use our skateboards as the wheels for the rolling stage. How we were going to have one person in front pulling the float with a bicycle and a dog. On the float will be the other guy portraying Washington surrounded by a couple of army privates. It was a sure winner. When Billy and I were done explaining our amazing idea, I looked up to see a big smile on each of our father's faces. Suddenly, we were surrounded by four dogs all wagging their tails in unison.

CHAPTER 10

The rest of that day was spent planning things out and discussing how we were going to take this project from an idea to reality. Billy and I went back and forth, writing down ideas on how to make the float work and what it should look like. Every once in a while, I would hear from Dash, Waldo, or Annie, putting their ideas in place or reminding us that they wanted to be included as well. When we broke for supper, we had the entire idea planned out, everything except who would portray Washington and who would be the muscle at the front on the bicycle.

"I think I should be Washington," Billy stated matter-of-factly. "I am the bigger of us two. I have more of a presidential look."

"I agree with you that you are bigger," I retorted. "And that makes you perfect for the muscle up front on the bike. We need strength up front. Someone that can pull this float throughout the whole parade route."

"I think the whole float should be pulled by dogs, much like in dog racing. But instead of a sled, we pull a rolling stage," Dash said proudly. "I can see it now, we will end up being in commercials just like those Clydesdale horses on all the cereal boxes, you watch. We'll be famous!"

I wanted to remind Dash that in order to be in the bicycle parade, we needed bicycles as part of the operation. But with Billy sitting two feet away from me, I could not just come right out and say it. I had to gingerly walk around his exclamation in a way that I would not sound like I was talking to an imaginary person. "Billy, we have to keep in mind this is a bicycle event. We are already taking a big chance in bringing in the float so we have to keep at least one bicycle up front pulling," I said out loud, hoping that would serve as a gentle reminder to Dash.

"Of course!" Billy snapped back. "Of course I remember we are entering a bicycle parade. Do you think this is the first time I have entered?" Billy was obviously getting upset with me. Dash could see it as well.

"Let's focus on the float build and how we are going to hook it up to the bicycle and assign parts closer to the Fourth," I said in an attempt to settle everyone's nerves. "We have nine days until showtime."

I looked at Billy who was drawing on a piece of paper and hoped that would stick with him. He kept drawing so I was convinced he would agree not to worry about parts just yet. I then glanced over at Dash who was nose down, sniffing around the door from inside the garage to the yard and following some sort of scent line. Waldo was laid out in front of the bucket that Billy was seated on while Annie and Hera were sprawled out in the grass not far from the fence that separated our yard from Doc Odell's. Although they were the Odell's dogs, Annie and Hera spent most of the days with me. Rarely did they spend much time inside. As Billy was drawing out his ideas for the parade float structure and how to make the connection to the bicycle, Doc Odell came out and asked what we were working on so intently.

"What are you two da Vinci's up to these days?" Doc inquired. "I have been watching you both and your merry band of canines for the past couple of hours. Something is up and I want in!"

"We can't say, Doc. You don't have high enough of a security clearance to be told," Billy said with a smile. "Super top secret plans for our Fourth of July parade float entry."

"Billy, quiet! You just gave away the main part of our idea!" I yelled across the yard.

"You tricked me, Doc!" Billy hollered. "You tricked me into telling you all about our parade float showing the crossing of the Pottowatomie River with Washington—"

"Billy!!" I yelled again, louder. "You keep making things worse and worse!"

But at this point, all four dogs were yelping and howling, "We are going to be pulling the float and acting like soldiers on the float. It's going to be great. There is no way any other kids can possibly win when we have four adorable dogs involved." Luckily, all Doc and Billy heard was dogs making quite the ruckus.

Annie got up and was running back and forth along the fence that Doc was leaned on and yelped, "I am going to pick up all of the dog treats people throw on the ground during parades. I am going to eat as much as I can." She was excitedly running back and forth.

"I am not sure what you said to get her all riled up," Doc said to no one in general, "but you sure do have her wound up! Try and settle her down a little bit before you boys go in tonight."

"Tell Doc not to worry, Max. I'll make sure that she's worn out before the streetlights come on and it is time to go to bed," Dash barked over to me.

"Don't worry, Doc. We will make sure she is tired out." I calmly said to Doc. "You have my word on that, even if that means I have to chase her myself."

"I can always count on you, Max. You and your family are great neighbors. One last thing, Max. Can you make sure that Annie does not dig in the dirt too much? Mrs. Odell said that Annie came in this afternoon with her paws covered in dirt. She said if she comes in with so much dirt on her paws one more time, Annie and Hera will not be able to come out and play with you anymore. Have a good night and just knock on the back door when Hera and Annie are ready to come in." With that statement, Doc went inside, leaving us all is shock.

"He didn't mean that, did he, Max?" inquired Dash. "Was he serious?"

"We can't lose Hera and Annie!" yelled Waldo. "They are half of our gang. They are a big piece of our pie."

Billy was just as surprised as the dogs. "Why would Doc say something like that? He knows that we are not doing it on purpose," he said with a small frown.

I agreed with everyone that Hera and Annie were a big part of our group. However, Annie would not go inside with dirty paws on purpose, but I did have to say that she has been covered in dirt lately.

I showed her what weeds to dig out. I also ran her through the mud a few times earlier this week when we were in the sprinkler.

Finally, Hera spoke up. "We need to pay more attention to making sure Annie's paws are clean and there is no evidence of digging as a group. We all know Annie is the best digger around, but if she goes inside full of mud again, the two of us will be stuck inside. We all have to work on keeping her clean and out of trouble."

As all the dogs were starting to walk around and wrestle with each other, Billy put down his drawings and said, "Annie and Hera are one of us. They are part of our team. We have to make sure we can continue to have them out with us. It just means that before we send them home, we need to do a paw check."

"I agree, Billy," I replied. "I know she can get into trouble sometimes and I really know that her ankle biting can be annoying, but she is part of our group. It will be up to us to make sure everyone is clean and ready to go back into the house." Both Billy and I were now standing next to the fence, surveying our empire. "After we check paws for dirt and mud, let's get Hera and Annie back to the Odell's and head for bed. The parade is nine days away from today, which only leaves us one week for the build. That should be enough time as long as nothing goes horribly wrong," I added, having no idea what the next week might hold. "What could possibly go wrong in a week?"

Over the next few days, Billy, the dogs, and I spent every waking hour together. After a few hours of debate and unsuccessful parade float mock-ups using action figures and matchbox cars, we finally came up with and agreed on a design and functional model. We had to ask our dads for help with some major float construction, including cutting the main piece of wood and connecting it to the skateboards we would be using as the wheels. We found some scrap wood to make the piece of plywood sturdy enough to support our weight, but light enough as to not smash or break our skateboards. Luckily, Billy's dad had an old rowboat out back behind their garage that had a large hole in the bottom.

"I never thought I would see the day when there was a use for this old thing again," Billy's dad said. "And never in a million years would I have ever thought that we would be fastening it to a piece of plywood bolted on some skateboards so that it could be pulled by dogs in a Fourth of July parade!"

"Me neither, Mike," my dad said proudly. "The boys are really carrying on the tradition of using their imaginations and building creations during the summers. Do you remember back when we were growing up and we invented that game? The one where we kicked the deflated volleyball over the fence and through broomsticks?" he asked loudly.

"Or when we modified the game of racquetball at the YMCA and convinced the investigative reporter from the local news program to come watch? How quickly he dismissed us!" Billy's dad said. "He looked so annoyed when he and the camera guy picked up and left. The boys sure are growing up fast."

As our fathers talked about the days when they were growing up, Billy and I were in the midst of a conversation of our own. Unfortunately, it was not going cordially. "I want to be Washington," Billy said sternly. "I am the bigger of the two of us. I should be the leader across the Pottowatomie."

"For the last time, it's Potomac, not Pottowatomie!" I yelled. "And if anyone is going to be Washington, it's me. I came up with the idea so I get to be the main character. Anyhow, you are the biggest so you need to be out front pulling the float."

"So what, now you are taking all the credit for thinking this idea up? I thought we both came up with the idea. Why do you get all the credit? Anyhow, the person up front will be on a bicycle and have one of the dogs next to him. Either one of us can pedal hard," snapped Billy. "If I do not get to be Washington, I am taking all my wood home with Waldo."

Dash, Waldo, Hera, and Annie all turned their heads to look over at us. This is the first time they had all heard us argue. "Are you two really going to let a silly Fourth of July parade come between such a good friendship?" remarked Hera. "You two have been friends, well, forever. I just can't see why this is that important to you."

Just as Hera was ending her sentence, our dads came in to see what all the yelling and barking was about. Neither Billy nor I wanted to admit to our dad's why we were arguing.

"Just tell them Annie was trying to wrestle with me and you two were breaking it up," Dash quickly yelped. "They do not need to know you two were arguing over something this stupid."

Once I began explaining that Annie was just acting foolish, both dads laughed and asked if we had tried to pull our contraption yet.

"No," stated Billy, "I guess we just figured it would be a cinch to pull. We have not designed or figured out how to connect the float to the bicycle just yet."

"I have been trying to sketch out a yolk, just like the oxen wagons in the old-fashioned days. Plus, we will need two connections, one for the bicycle and one for the dog," I said matter-of-factly. I was trying to sound as grown-up and smart as I could.

"I think you two need to work on getting the power hooked up. This is already a hefty project and no one is on the float yet," my dad said. "Here, Mike, let's hook up a rope to the back if Billy's bicycle and drill a hole through the plywood to wrap a leash through. I think the boys need to feel just how heavy this is going to be." With our dads' help, we were able to get the float out onto the driveway and hooked up in less than an hour.

As Billy hooked Dash up to the leash that was fed through the cutout, I grabbed the second rope and then helped Billy onto the bike. "On the count of three, start pulling," said Billy. "One, two, three!" And away we went—or so I thought. I ran in place, pulling as hard as I could. Dash was clawing to get some traction on the concrete, but all I heard was his nails scraping across with each stride. Billy was the only one making any headway on moving but he was just barely making his tires spin. "Mush! Mush!" yelled Billy at the top of his lungs.

"Pull harder, pull harder!" Annie barked as loud as she could.

"Faster, faster!" Waldo yelled, now starting to laugh at the lack of any real progress.

"I think this boat is sunk even before it leaves the harbor," Dash said to me, just as he was moving toward me to give my hand a reassuring lick. "Not all things are meant to be. At least you found out soon enough to be able to decorate your bikes for the parade." I disconnected Dash from the leash so that he could run around. I then looked up to see Billy in the same spot he was when he was pedaling as hard as he could.

"I just wanted to win first prize, Max," Billy said. "I just wanted to be the center of attention. I wanted to be the winner. I wanted something that was for just me. I am never first. Since my mom died, everything in my life has changed. I . . . I just want to win at something." I did not know what to say. I have never seen Billy like this. He was always so happy and cheerful. As I was looking down and petting Dash, not really knowing what to say, Billy said, "I'll see you tomorrow. I think I want to sleep in my own bed tonight." With that, he and Waldo slowly made their way down the driveway to go home.

Dash and I sat outside, thinking for a little bit. "Life has changed for him, Max. Life will never be the same like it was before. He is right," Dash said. I was still trying to let everything that happened that day sink in. I tried to put myself in Billy's shoes. I am not sure how long I was staring off into space when Dash broke the silence. "We need to give Billy a chance at winning. We have to make this parade the best ever so that he can be the winner. If he wants to be George Washington, then we need to find a way to get that boat across the Potomac." Just then, my mom opened up the screen door and told us it was time for bed and to make sure to brush my teeth and clean behind my ears. "Do humans really get that much dirt behind their ears?" Dash asked. "It seems like a person would really have to work on getting dirt there."

"Dash, I think that is one of those questions that will perplex mankind for generations to come, just like why do bad things happen to good people."

It was one of the few nights of the summer that Dash and I did not play Uno just before falling asleep. But just like every other night that summer and beyond, I fell asleep with my best buddy curled up next to me. Best friends forever.

CHAPTER 12

As the days passed by, Billy, the dogs, and I kept working on making our parade float a success. We decided that my bicycle would be used to pull the float. I would pedal as hard as I could while Dash would be connected to the float as well by his harness from his collar to my handlebars. Billy would be standing in the front of the boat dressed as George Washington. Waldo would be sitting in the rear of the boat with Hera and Annie on the sides, depicting revolutionary soldiers. My bicycle was fully decorated in red, white, and blue streamers and ribbons. We cut out the waves, painted them with whitecaps, and secured them to the boards so that when I hit the brakes, the waves slid back and forth. The float was looking perfect. My mom took measurements of Billy and sewed a coat that could have been used in 1776. We even made Billy a wig made from white yarn. We had everything covered. With only four days left to go, we had everything covered to help Billy get his first big "win" in life. Or so we thought.

It was late morning Saturday when we decided that we needed to give the whole float another test ride. Billy and I had a secret meeting to determine if we needed the dry run. "The float looks perfect, Max," Billy said calmly. "We have thought of everything and have all of our bases covered." I was letting that statement sink in, trying to think of what else could go wrong, when I started to hear the low grumble of bark.

"It's too heavy," I heard from what seemed like across the country. "There is no way we can pull that float, especially with Billy and his soldiers on it. There is just too much weight." I finally heard enough of what was being said to realize it was Dash talking to me. "We have to give it a test run today so we can make adjustments as needed. But just by looking at the float, we will not be able to budge it more than an inch. And that inch is only because the driveway slopes downhill," Dash said matter-of-factly. "If we want to make this a sure victory, we need more humans."

"Humans are the last thing I want to bring into this," I replied back to Dash, not thinking at all about who else might hear me talking to a dog. "The more people that we get involved, the more people there are that might steal our idea. Look at how hard we have worked on this project since the first day. Do you want someone to come in and steal our idea?" I said, my voice getting louder and louder the more I was aggravated. "There's no way I am going to ask any other boys—or girls, for that matter—we know to help. It's just out of the question. I would think that you knew me better than that." I ended that statement with stomping my foot and folding my arms across my chest.

"Well, I am not sure what to say," Billy said, sheepishly. "Honestly, I wasn't going to suggest anyone our age to help at all. I was not even thinking that it was too heavy, Max, honest. I'm sorry if I got you upset, and you sure are, but I sure didn't mean to. I would never ever try to purposefully get you mad."

"Aw, Bill, it's not you," I said, backtracking a little bit. "You know, I just get so involved in things." How could I explain to Billy that I was upset and mad at something my dog said as I was talking to him! "Billy, let's see how heavy this is and how far we can pull it. The parade route is long, almost four blocks long, so if we get tired here in the driveway, there will be no way we can manage the entire length of the parade," I told him. "We just need to make a dry run here on the driveway."

We agreed on pushing the parade float out of the garage and just past the door. I would then hook up Billy's bicycle (as mine was already decorated perfectly) and get Dash connected. After the front end was secure, Billy would get Waldo to sit in the rear and Hera and Annie on the sides. Neither one of us had given any thought to the difficulty of such a task, getting three dogs to sit perfectly still on a rocking and swaying piece of plywood loosely screwed on four skateboards pulled by a underpowered bicycle and a single dog.

After everyone and everything was hooked up, I looked back, saw the thumbs up, and heard a loud yell "Let's go!" from Billy.

I pedaled as hard as I could. My eyes were closed as I could feel my legs pumping away. I opened my eyes for just a moment and saw the back tire spinning. I was so happy we were moving! The faster I pumped and pedaled, the faster I was able to see the rear tire move. "Dash, this is going to be great!" I exclaimed to my buddy next to me. "We're going to win all five blue ribbons this year! How could anyone not vote for us across the board?" I asked my trusted canine again.

"Well, there is one big problem," I heard. I was still pumping and pedaling as fast as I could, but I was a little perplexed because instead of Dash's voice, I heard what sounded like Billy's. "You can probably stop pedaling," I was told just as I felt the tap on my right shoulder. "We are in bigger trouble than I think either one of us ever figured," the Billy sounding voice said again. "Max, stop pedaling. We are too heavy," Billy said to me as I slowly opened my eyes. "We have not moved even an inch. The dogs stayed on the float stayed put perfectly. In the beginning, Dash did great but sat down once he saw that we were not moving anywhere. Look, you left a skid mark on the driveway from where your tire was spinning in place. We are in deep now." Billy was just telling me how he saw the scene behind me when I was pedaling. He was right, we did not move an inch.

"Now what?" inquired Waldo from his spot in the rowboat.

"I'm not sure if this helps or not," Annie commented, "But the waves worked great with each of your leg pumps. They were swaying back and forth. It was actually starting to make me a little seasick watching them!"

"I think it is time that we hang this idea up," Dash said to me frankly. "We can still take this all apart and make sure that your bicycles are decorated for the parade. Nothing lost now, except some time, but even that was not lost. It was a fun for all of us to work together."

"Not going to happen," I said again somewhat aggravated. "We started this project and we are going to see it to completion. I can't even believe that you even suggested that we quit."

"I am starting to think that you have an imaginary friend, Max," Billy said to me dryly and sternly. "This is the second time in twenty minutes that you are talking to another person when it's only the two of us and the dogs. Or can you translate a dogs' bark into English?" With that silly suggestion, Billy had ten eyes immediately trained on him.

"Do you think he knows?" asked Annie shyly.

"How could he have found out?" Hera replied to Annie.

"Know what?" Waldo said nervously, thinking about all the times we had talked about Billy without his knowledge.

"Settle down, canines. Settle down. There's no way Billy knows. Why would he pick this moment to make it known? He was just putting a question out there as something funny," Dash said, looking over at me for any sign that might back up his ideas.

"I think we are all good," I blurted out. "I don't think anyone around here is any wiser about any secrets we have going on," I said to no one in particular. "We just really need to find more power. But where are we going to find what we need this close to the Fourth of July? Especially someone or something that is not already planning on entering the parade?"

"We need people," Billy stated. "We need big people. We need strong people. Most of all, we need honest people. People that will not come in for a few days, get all of our secrets and plans in their minds, write them down, sneak away, and then build their own dog-powered General Washington-crossing-the-Pottowatomie-parade float."

At this point, it was almost in perfect unison that we all yelled at Billy, "It's not the Pottowatomie, it's the Potomac River!"

As his cheeks started to turn red out of embarrassment, I had the answer flash before my eyes.

CHAPTER
13

I darted down the driveway to the curb, yelling, "I'll be right back. Don't let the dogs loose. I will be back in a jiffy." I ran up to the curb, looking both ways to cross. I was always told that I had to come to a complete stop at the curb to make sure that I did not dart out in front of any traffic or pop out between cars. After looking both ways, I was back into a dead sprint up our driveway, through the back gates, into the kitchen door, and up the stairs to Maggie's room. I could hear that she and Grace were in there based on the music volume and the amount of girly giggles.

"What do you want, cheese breath?" she asked even before I had knocked. "I told you never to bother me when my door was closed, when I had company, especially when my door is closed *and* I have company!"

"I need your help," I asked quietly. "We need your help with our Fourth of July parade float."

"Your Fourth of July what?" Maggie asked, equally annoyed that I was bothering Grace and her on a Saturday afternoon and asking for her assistance. "There are no floats in the parade. The parade is for kids. Young kids like you and Billy. Floats are meant for regular parades. Parades where people watch for news program to host the event or for Miss America. Since you are none of the above—" extolled my sister Maggie.

"Butt out!" yelled Grace, interrupting.

"But . . . but . . . but . . ." I stammered. I was not able to get any more words out before they were back in unison.

"Exactly! You're learning something in school," both girls said in perfect step. "See, you know what we're going to say before we even need to say it. Now get out of here and take your fleabag friends out of here. There's no way we're going to help you two cheese breaths do anything." And with that, the door was slammed shut in my face.

I turned around to make the long walk back to Billy's garage, dejected that I was told no way but happy in knowing that I was rejected alone. I now had to come up with some excuse to give Billy why they said no. I did not want Billy to know what they said. I did not want Billy to know that Maggie and her friend did not want to help him get his first real victory in life. In all honesty, deep down, I really did not want Billy to know just how mean my sister could be. Well, until I went to take the first step down the stairs, that is. On that first step was Billy and each step below were the four dogs. Each sitting on their own step, looking to me for answers. They all looked at me with puppy dog eyes and sadness.

"Now what?" questioned Annie, the smallest of the group. "I hope that Maggie and Grace were not the only option. It sure sounded like they meant it when they said no."

"Does this mean that we are out of the parade?" asked Waldo. "I've always wanted to be in the parade. Every year we just get to sit on the grass next to the curb, waiting for you to come by on your bicycles. All the streamers and ribbons flowing in the gentle summer breeze. I thought this was the year we would all be involved."

"I think we are sunk," Hera said dryly. "Our boat to success sank before we even made it out of the surf." She was looking straight ahead with a glazed over look. "Back to being spectators."

"I have faith!" Dash exclaimed loudly. "I have full faith in—"

"SHUT THAT FLEABAG UP!" Maggie screamed at me as the door to her room was flung open. "My finger is already on speed dial to Mom. Do you really want to miss your precious parade over one of your four-legged noisemakers barking in the house? What are all of these dogs doing in here anyway? Benji is trying to take his afternoon nap. You're going to be in so much trouble!" she bemoaned, smiling as she closed the door again.

"If I didn't know your sister any better," Billy said shyly, "I would say that she enjoyed yelling at us. I wish that we could figure out a way to get Maggie and Grace to help us. They are much so bigger than us and a hundred times more powerful. They would be perfect to help pull the float!"

"Can you figure out a way to make that happen, Max?" Waldo said excitedly.

"Yeah, can you sweet-talk them into helping?" Annie yelped.

"It will take some thinking," I replied to the crew as we were on our way out the kitchen door. "I'm going to have to think fast and quick. The parade starts Wednesday at noon. Today is Saturday. Four days away. I'll try and think of a solution this afternoon. If by Tuesday morning there is no hope in our parade float entry idea working out, then we all agree to pack everything up and start to decorate Billy's bike for a solo entry into the parade," I said, hoping for a six-way agreement.

"Agreed!" everyone barked in complete unison.

"OK," I said quickly. "All we have to do now is convince my sister and her best friend that pulling a piece of plywood painted to look like a river with an old worn-out rowboat on top and one soon-to-be fifth grader standing on it surrounded by four dogs, which is loosely bolted to four skateboards and pulled by a bicycle is a great way to spend a portion of their summer!" I announced as matter-of-factly as I could, but I started to laugh as soon as the words crossed my lips, which was perfect because Billy was already laughing and the dogs were mid chortle halfway through my speech.

CHAPTER 14

Supper at our house was one of the only times during the day where everyone in our family actually saw and talked to one another. As long as we were all home, we ate together. Anyone else around would be invited and welcomed as well, which is to say if we had any friends over at the house who would like to eat, they could. Billy and I were going to use this family practice to convince Maggie and Grace that we truly needed their help. The Bookers eat supper at 5:00 p.m. every day. That time does not waiver. If we were fifteen minutes late, then it is very likely that we missed supper. Looking at our watches indicated that we had just over an hour to come up with and hatch our parade plan.

Billy was just spitting out suggestions as quickly as they came into his head. "Tell them there is a money prize if we win and they can keep it," Billy tossed out as an idea.

"What happens if we do win?" I asked. "Then where do we come up with the prize money? You and I do not earn enough in weekly allowance to entice Maggie."

"Can we bribe her with the promise of doing her chores?" Billy inquired. "No one likes to pick up laundry or vacuum the floors."

"Listen, Bill, I want to win as much as the next guy, but let's not go nutty with the chore ideas here," I remarked. "I already have enough to do every week by picking up after Dash in the yard. Plus, at the beginning of this summer, Doc Odell started paying me to pick up after Hera and Annie. I'm up to my ankles in doggie doo. I don't think adding more chores to my life is the right plan."

With that, Billy and I were back to thinking out loud and tossing a Frisbee back and forth while Dash and the other dogs were going through their own ideas for the help. "What we need to find out, is something that will guarantee Maggie and her friend want to be in the parade," Waldo said to Hera. "If we can find something that they like and enjoy, they will be asking Max to help."

"If Maggie thinks that she is going to benefit from helping the boys, then the hard part is over!" exclaimed Hera.

"What are the girls interested in?" questioned Annie. "Does anyone know what has the power to pull those two out of Maggie's room away from her computer and radio?" I was starting to hear the commotion from the dogs so my ears perked up.

"Hold it," Dash said loudly. "I know how to make Maggie and Grace work with us." The others began to yelp and howl louder and louder. "Boys," Dash added calmly and without much excitement. "The only thing that is a sure fire guarantee to get those two interested in the parade is boys."

"That's it!!" I yelled at the top of my lungs. "Boys!" I screamed, jumping up and down while running, skipping, and hopping over to Billy. "If we can figure out a way to make Maggie think that boys will be at the parade, then she and Grace will definitely want to help us."

Billy looked at me and then over toward the dogs who were all up and excitedly chasing after one another. "You sure did get them all riled up quick with that brilliant idea," he said while chucking the Frisbee back in my direction. "I'm not sure if Maggie will think boys are a good enough idea, but Dash and Waldo sure do. I don't think it will work, but if you do, let's try it. I mean, if they had a parade float and needed our help, trying to get us to help them would surely not work if they got even *more* girls involved. That would make me want to help even less," Billy noted.

"I'm not sure why, but those two talk about boys constantly," I told Billy, giving him a little more insight to my sister's life. "Maggie and Grace spend a huge part of their day talking about, looking at, or talking to boys. We just need to find the names of the right ones and then try and lure them into our plan."

"Which boys we know are going to work?" Billy questioned. "I don't think any of our friends will do the trick. Hank's magic is amazing, but I don't think Maggie will think he is as talented as we do. Dominic's trombone playing and school spirit makes everyone smile and tap their toes, but I just don't think Gracie will agree," Billy said with a hint of skepticism in his voice. "I really think this is a good idea but we don't have the time or the knowledge to make it work. I'm starting to lose faith that we will be able to get our parade float to the start line." I could see it in Billy's face that he was defeated. I could hear it in his voice that he had lost all hope.

Just as I was about to reassure him that all was well and we had destiny on our side, Mom hollered out the kitchen window, "Suppertime, fellas! Come and get it!"

Dash was up in an instant, plodding his way toward the house. Hera and Annie raced toward the gate, allowing them back into Doc's yard so they could eat supper as well. I started to make my way to the kitchen door when Billy said, "I think I am going to eat at home tonight. I am not too hungry and would like some time alone." I didn't know what to say. Billy had never wanted to be alone or at least he never said it out loud. I asked if he was positive, to which he replied, "Yep, just need a bit of time to think."

"OK," I yelled to him as he slowly ambled his way down the drive.

Dash and I stood and watched as Billy walked down to the curb where Waldo sat. Billy looked left, right, and then left again before he crossed the street. He must have known or felt that we were staring at him because as soon as he got to the other side, he raised his right arm and hand up, waving it above his head, and went straight into his house. Dash and I were left outside alone.

"Max," Dash said sternly to me, "we have to figure out a way to make this Fourth of July parade be the best one ever."

"I know, Dash," I replied, already knowing what he said was the truth. "I know. If we only knew what would make Maggie and Grace excited."

It was just a couple of minutes past five as we made our way inside. If we wanted to have something to eat, we needed to wash up and quickly sit down at the table.

CHAPTER 15

There are few rules in our house that are set in stone. If you made the mess, you clean up the mess. No one is allowed to eat off my dad's plate. And Saturday night is pizza night. Always. Before I was born, my mom stayed at home with Maggie and my dad volunteered as a firefighter on his days off from the zoo. He often tells us how they would weave in and out of traffic with lights flashing and sirens blaring, going to help someone or some family in their time of need. He would tell us about how much fun it was to wrestle hoses into burning buildings or cut open cars like tuna cans after vehicular accidents. He did this as a way to give back to our small community. Saturday nights were traditionally pizza night at the fire houses so that tradition was carried on in our house even after Mom went back to writing and reporting about the news of the day.

When I was washing my hands and face in the powder room, I heard the doorbell ring, the door opening and closing, and then the screams and giggles of two teenaged girls.

"OMG, Maggie!" screamed Grace. "He is totally adorbs."

"I can imagine it now," Maggie chimed in, "Mrs. Edward Huffnagle. It rolls off the tongue so seamlessly. That would be a perfect world, Gracie, total and complete perfection." She had a glossed-over look in her eyes as she came into the kitchen and placed the pizza box in the middle of the table.

"You're so right, Maggie," Grace replied with her own far-off stare. "The only problem is, Teddy has no idea who we are. He's going to be a senior. We're only entering our sophomore year."

"Wait, who is Teddy?" asked Dash. "I'm so confused. I thought the pizza bringer's name was Edward. Are they not in love with him anymore? Have they dropped pizza guy Edward already and moved on to this pizza guy Teddy?"

"Teddy is a nickname for Edward," I answered Dash's question. As soon as I said it, I knew I made a mistake. I was talking to a dog when I was surrounded by my family.

"Buzz off, cheddar breath," Maggie told me as she tossed a dish towel at my head. "Who invited you and Mr. Fleabags here to eat with us anyhow?"

"Don't you have a big wheel or scooter to decorate for the silly parade on Wednesday?" Gracie said. "We are talking about adult stuff, not kid problems, like what happens if it rains and the streamers on your bike get wet." That example made both of the girls laugh out loud as well as my trusted best friend, Dash.

"It's funny to think about a big pile of wet paper streamers," Dash said. "How all the colored dye runs out and the sidewalk is stained for weeks."

"All right, everyone. Let's all go to our corners and settle down," Mom said in an attempt to have at least one meal a week without an argument. "If we can't all eat in peace, then maybe we need to start having family only suppers." Both Maggie and I understood what that meant so we all sat down in our seats to eat peacefully.

"Was that Teddy Huffnagle?" my Dad asked, having not heard the girls melting away in love. "He sure has grown up from when his father would bring him by the firehouse to climb on the rigs and pull the air horn. He was a really cute kid. Almost as cute as my little *schmoopy*."

"DAD! I have told you a billion times to stop calling me that!" exclaimed my sister at the top of her lungs. "I hate it!"

"Settle down, Margaret, settle down," my Mom chimed in. We both knew that if we were called by our real first names, it was the first verbal warning. If our first names were used with our middle name—or initial, in my case—that was strike two *and* three all in one.

"Sorry, Mom. He just gets me so aggravated sometimes! I hate that name," Maggie said, a little embarrassed she was called that and then scolded in front of her friend.

"And, Dave, you need to start giving her a little more respect now that she is growing older. Agreed?" my mom asked, giving us all a once-over through her glare.

"Yes, Mom," we all agreed in unison.

"Mr. Booker, you know the Huffnagle family?" Gracie inquired openly, taking another piece of pizza out of its box. "Do the Bookers know everyone in town?"

"Well, I'm not sure about everyone, but we defiantly know the Huffnagle family. Mike Rhu, Billy's dad across the street, and I went to school with Pete Huffnagle. When we graduated college, Pete and I were hired by the fire department here in town. Very soon after I left the job, Pete was elected mayor. And the rest, as they say, is history!" my dad said, sounding somewhat proud of the notion that he was friends with the mayor. As he went on explaining the trials and tribulations of growing up with the now mayor, Dash started to make his famous barfing noises.

"Take Dash outside right away," Mom said to me while scooting back from the table to give me access to Dash. "The last thing I need tonight is to be cleaning up after him having eaten too much grass. Out, out, out!"

"Come on, Dash, let's get you outside," I said, grabbing a piece of pizza for the road. "I really have no idea what you could have gotten into!"

When we were safely outside and out of the hearing range of anyone, Dash looked up and said, "That's it, Max! That's how we get Maggie and Grace to help us. When we go back inside, gently remind them who does the judging of the bicycles in the parade and that his family always sits on the stage platform with him. They will be asking us to help."

"It won't work, Dash," I told him, thinking there was no way they would want to help us. "Maggie and Grace are in their own little world. No way would they want to help two almost ten-year-olds work on such a silly project. Are you feeling any better? I want to go in and get more pizza before they eat it all."

"Yeah, okay, let's go back in. If you don't think it will work, then we will have to figure something else out. I thought this would work, which is why I faked being sick so we could talk," Dash said, obviously upset that I had not latched on to his notion of them wanting to help us faster. We trudged across the yard and were climbing the stairs into the back door when all of a sudden, both Maggie and Grace came flying out the door, tackling me into the grass.

"What the heck was that for?" I squawked like a bird. "Why would you tackle me like that? It hurt and I almost fell on Dash! What gives?"

"Dad told us that you were doing something a little more unique this year than just decorating your bicycles for the parade. He also said that you might have a couple of openings for the two prettiest high school sophomores you know," Maggie screamed into my face while sitting on my stomach and holding me down.

"We want to help, you know, to win the parade. We want you, Billy, and Sir Fleabags over there to be champs," Grace said, trying to wrestle my shoes off to tickle my feet.

"We know how much this means to you, and I always want to see you succeed and win at stuff so this is a perfect arrangement," Maggie continued.

"It has nothing to do with the fact that Mr. Huffnagle is judging and Teddy will be right there with him," Grace piggybacked on Maggie's sentence. "We are just, you know, thinking of you two!"

"See, Max," Dash said smugly, "I tried to tell you!"

I struggled to get loose and stand up. I was not sure which was worse, knowing that in order to get what I wanted for Billy my sister's help was needed or that getting my sister's help would mean the stinky Dash was right. Either way, I had a feeling in my stomach that four nights from now, I would be walking around with at least one blue ribbon pinned to my shirt.

CHAPTER 16

Maggie, Grace, Dash, and I made our way across the street. I knocked on the door but no one answered. Waldo looked out the kitchen window and barked, "They went out to the movies, Max. They won't be back until later tonight."

"That dog is always barking at everyone that goes by," Maggie said harshly. "He sure does not seem to be a friendly dog."

"Aw, he's not that bad," I said in defense of our four-legged friend. "He's just trying to protect his house." I led the two newcomers to the rear and opened up the garage, showing them our parade production. Their eyes almost popped out of their head's when they saw what lay in front of them.

"How is this an entry for a bicycle parade, Max?" inquired Maggie. "What I see here is one bicycle, four skateboards with a piece of plywood attached, and a rowboat with a hole in it!" Her interest was lessening with every moment she was staring at what we had accomplished.

"Hold on, let me explain. The parade does not have any rules attached to it. Traditionally, only bicycles have entered because no one has ever thought of anything but bicycles! What is more patriotic than a scene right out of the Revolutionary War," I said, trying to plead my case. "What better way to grab your boyfriend's attention than to show up on the most well-thought-out entry in the whole *shebang!*" I could tell that Maggie and Grace were skeptical.

"Tell them they can have costumes if they want," Dash remarked, nudging my hand with his nose. "Tell them that they will get to pull the float with us two up front."

"Where do you think we are going to fit in this debacle?" asked Maggie.

"Yeah, where exactly is there space on the float for us both?" Grace inquired. "Obviously, one of us with be George Washington, but who will the other person be? I don't remember Mrs. Washington making the trip with George."

"Well, I agree that there is really only space for one person on the float," I replied in total and complete agreement with both of their observations. "Billy is going to be Washington. He already has his costume made and fitted. We have also trained Waldo to be in the back of the boat. We were hoping that maybe, just maybe, you two could—"

"I'm not pulling this contraption," they both said in perfect unison as if practiced for weeks prior. "Nope!"

Dash and I could see our parade float setting sail into the sea of failure even before we were able to get the main sail up. I had to think fast and figure out a way to at least not have them quit that night. "Tell them that we were thinking about showcasing them up front. That way, they could pull the float and still toss out candy by themselves! What better way to get the attention of a high school boy than through candy!" Dash howled wildly. I immediately told that to the girls, which they did not outright reject.

"I think that might be OK," Maggie said in agreement. "If we can have enough candy to hand out over the entire parade route, this just might work."

"Yeah, like, we can have extra bags on the stage behind the waves, and you can bring them up to us when we run out," Grace said, pointing at me. "You can be like the little bugler in the army."

I did not want to remind them that I was probably going to be on my bicycle during the parade, hooked up to both Dash and the float while pedaling as hard as I could. I knew better than that. At this point in my life, I knew when I had to quit while I was ahead. As I closed the garage door down behind us, I started to get the feeling that this Fourth of July parade might just work out and be the best part of my entire life. All we had to do practice a few times and then make it until noon on Wednesday. How hard could that be, right?

CHAPTER 17

"**I** don't think that you want to wake up and go downstairs," I vaguely heard while dreaming about Washington crossing the Potomac. "I think we should try and stay up here as long as we can. We can order pizzas and have Maggie bring us peanut butter and jelly sandwiches," I heard ever more clearly as I was opening up my eyes and realizing what was actually happening. "If you keep your head down and your eyes closed, maybe your mom will forget what happened by the time you wake up," Dash was whispering as low as he could in my ear. When I fully opened my eyes, Dash's snout was resting on the edge of my bed, directly in front of my face, mere inches away. "Bad news, Max. The worst," he said again.

My mind raced through all the possibilities that it could be, given the situation. I convinced myself that my family was all OK, as I did not think that my parents would rely on a dog who did not know that I understood his barks to break any bad news to me. I could hear my mom and dad downstairs talking to each other, but they did not seem to be shouting at one another. I strained my ears to see if I could make out any of the words they were saying, but couldn't. "I give up, Dash, what happened?" I inquired. "Is this goldfish-dead bad or left-my-baseball-glove-out-in-the-rain bad?" Dash knew my level of bad was on a sliding scale. I trusted his assessment of the situation.

"Your-mom's-flowerbed-was-torn-apart-and-dug-up-overnight bad. The gate to Doc Odell's yard was open. It sounds like Annie is to blame. Your mom told your dad that Annie was not allowed to come over anymore if Doc is not around," Dash solemnly told me. "We're not allowed to play with her anymore." I could tell in Dash's voice that this was not a joke. There was a whimper in that last part when he said that we won't be allowed to play with Annie anymore. I was not sure what to do. This was not directly my fault. In fact, I had nothing to do with this. But the reality was that Annie was a close friend of mine and an even closer friend to my best friend, Dash.

"Don't worry, Dash," I tried to reassure him. "You worry too much. Let's go downstairs and see what happened. My mom is reasonable and, more importantly, as an investigative journalist, she will get to the bottom of this mystery."

Both Dash and I made our way downstairs after I brushed my teeth and put on clean clothes. It was Sunday after all. I slowly and quietly made my way into the kitchen when I heard, "Max T., please come in here and bring Dash with you." Mom had used my middle initial. Things were worse that I originally thought. "When the girls and you came back home last night from the Rhus, did you happen to notice anything unusual about the front garden?" she asked me. I felt like I was being questioned in the police station under one of those big lights like they show on TV.

"No, Mom, why? Everything looked just as it did the other day after we weeded," I replied with confidence that if I just answered honestly, all would be forgiven.

"Ah, yes, the day you were weeding," she said with a bit more of an angry tone than before. "Who helped you dig out all of those weeds? It sure was a big job, and from what Mr. Rhu tells me, Billy was at the dentist's office, leaving you alone."

"*Ummm*, yes, I was alone," I blurted out. "Well, sort of alone. I was people alone, but not friend alone. Dash, Waldo, Hera, and Annie helped me. With them all pitching in, the job went by quick! Even Dad said it looked great." I was back thinking this would end on a positive note.

"Yes, so I have heard. You were using the dogs to help you dig out the weeds. How were you 'training' them to know what was a weed and what was a flower, Max?" she inquired again, this time sounding angrier than before. "How were you able to show them flowers versus weeds?"

I was stumped. How could I explain that I could talk to Dash and all the other dogs? How could I tell her that I just showed them and they would know? I mean, at this point, if I pull out the "I can talk to dogs" routine, I'm going to be grounded for the rest of the summer, including the parade in what was now just three short days away. Three short days that we needed to practice with the new addition of two crew members!

"I think what your mother is trying to tell you, Max, is that the entire garden was dug up overnight. All of her award-winning flowers were dug up and dumped on the grass. Earlier this year, we put some flakes down on the dirt so that no other animals would want to go near the flower bed," my dad explained to me. "We are almost positive that it was not raccoons or possums. Dash was inside with you last night. We called across the street to find out that Waldo was also inside. The paw marks in the dirt are too small for Hera. So that leaves only one dog that could be the culprit."

"It can't be Annie!" I screamed at them. "It can't be! Annie is a good girl! Sure, she gets into trouble every now and then and loves to chase Hera and chomp on her ears and maybe even bite a person's ankle sometimes, but—" With that *but*, I stopped. The more I talked about Annie, the more it sounded like I was only saying bad things that she does. "I . . . I . . . I . . ." I stammered, "I just don't think it was her."

"Since there is no way to truly find out whether she did this or not, Max, we think it's best if Annie stays in Doc's yard when he is not around," my dad said. "I can see that you are upset, but your mom puts a lot of work and effort into her garden so it is not fair that it was dug up. I'm sorry, buddy, but this has to happen." Dad went to hug me before walking into the kitchen and asking what I wanted for breakfast.

"Nothing, I'm not hungry," I replied.

"I understand you're upset, but if you do get hungry, come inside. OK?" he asked.

"Sure," I replied, knowing full well I was not going to be hungry enough to eat ever again. Dash and I slunk out the kitchen door to the backyard, forced to hear my mom dragging the garbage cans down the driveway to clean up after the flower massacre. "Do you think Annie could have done this, Dash?" I asked my four-legged friend.

"I sure hope not, Max. I sure hope not. But if you start to list all of the things that Annie does get into, this does not fall far from that tree," Dash said, slowing down his pace knowing that we were going to be able to see in Doc Odell's yard soon.

As soon as we came around the corner of our house, we were able to see Hera and Annie sitting in their yard and looking through the fence. They looked like two prisoners sentenced to jail for the rest of their lives. "What happened?" Hera asked.

"That's what we want to know, Annie," Dash exclaimed. "Did you dig up all of the flowers in the garden?"

"Of course not, Dash! I can't believe that you would even think that!" Annie bellowed back. "How dare you even mention it! We were inside together all night. The only time that I was not next to Hera snuggled up on our bed was when I came out in the middle of the night to go potty. Other than that, we were sleeping!"

"Hera, do you agree with Annie?" asked Dash. "Was she right there with you all night?"

"Yes, yes, she was." Hera replied softly. "But I just don't know how we can not only prove Annie did not do it, but also show your mom who did do it."

"Leave that up to Billy and me," I excitedly told the assembled gang of canines. I think I have a plan.

CHAPTER 18

With Annie on virtual lockdown, I headed over to Billy's to explain the current situation. As I knocked, I could see through the screen door that he was just finishing up breakfast with his dad. Under the table lay a very comfortable looking Waldo. I gave the door our secret rap. Tap, tap, knock! I saw Billy's eyes light up and look straight at me.

"We have trouble, Billy," I said quite matter-of-factly.

"I know," said Billy in a quick response. "We heard what happened overnight. Your dad called to make sure that Waldo was not involved in the destruction. Luckily, my dad said that since I had a rough day yesterday, Waldo could spend the night inside. Boy am I ever glad he did!"

As Billy put his dirty dishes into the sink, his dad tapped him on the head and reminded him, "Try not to get into too much trouble today!"

"We won't, Dad. I promise," Billy replied.

The three of us headed back over to my side of the street, waiting at the curb for a car to pass, then looking left and right and left again. "Can't be too cautious about safety," I said to Billy in my best Mr. Hartl impression. Mr. Hartl was our gym and health teacher who always talked in his own style. Anytime we would say or do anything health or safety related, it just sounded better in Mr. Hartl's voice.

Walking up the driveway, I heard some voices I was not expecting this early on a Sunday morning. "Are we going to have rehearsal or what, Gouda breath? We need to make sure this performance is one to remember forever!" Maggie said in her best rich person impression.

"Yeah," Grace tacked on, "Like we need to be perfect for Teddy."

"We have a problem, Maggie," I told her bluntly. "Mom's garden was dug up and she is blaming Annie. She told us that Annie was not allowed to come out of Doc's yard if Doc is not around. That means we are one dog short for the float."

"Two dogs short, Max. You are two dogs short," Hera said, laying on her back on the concrete and soaking up the sun. "With Annie being wrongly accused of destroying the garden, then I am out as well. Until Annie is once again free to roam and play, then I am staying in here with her!"

"Isn't that just peachy keen," Dash said to me. "Now we are down two team members, Max. What are we going to do?" It was obvious to me that Dash was nervous about the parade, but much more nervous about our friends.

"Can you please get them all to stop barking, Max?" Maggie said. "All this noise is bad for our skin. We won't be able to participate in this parade if the stress level is constantly this high."

"I understand, everyone," I said, hoping to use the broadest of verbal brushstrokes so that everyone I knew would be covered. "I think the best thing that we can do right now is have the girls go inside and work on their walking costumes. Remember, 1776 is the key."

"Right on, Max," replied Grace. "We will have our costumes designed by lunch and we can start to put it all together this afternoon."

"Great!" shouted Maggie. "I will then be able to take over as not only creative director, but also as director of what happens on the stage." I did not have the energy just then to argue with her, although Billy, Waldo, and Dash all looked at me for reassurance that she was not going to be running the entire float.

"Just let her think whatever she wants for right now," I whispered to anyone that was near me. "Just let her think that until after lunch, we have bigger issues to contend with." Which was true, we did have bigger issues. One half of our canine stage crew was on permanent lockdown and false imprisonment for something that she may not have done. We needed to find the identity of the true flower digger.

CHAPTER
19

We all sat next to the fence. Billy, Waldo, Dash, and I were on our side, while Hera and Annie were on the Odell's side. There was not much that could be said. I must admit, the evidence did point toward Annie. I did just teach her this past week how to dig up flowers and weeds. She did have a history of digging in the grass or dirt. Lastly, the gate to her yard was left open for my dad to find this morning when he walked out to get the paper.

"How are we going to solve this, Max?" Billy asked with a slight tremble in his voice. "I wish we could just ask her if she dug up the flowers." The trembling was getting worse and worse.

"What good would that do us?" I asked Billy. "If we could talk to her and she answered that she did not do it, it would not get us any closer to where we were now." I said this somewhat sternly. When I glanced over at Billy, he had his head resting on Waldo's chest and belly, staring up to the heavens. Dash was soaking up the sun while lying on the grass directly next to the fence. Hera and Annie were doing the same on the walkway, leading from the fence gate to the back door of the Odell's house. "There has to be some sort of clue as to what happened and who did it."

"It is times like this that I wish I had read more detective books from the library. They always go over how they solved the puzzles, but I usually just skip to the conclusion," admitted Billy. "I don't have the patience to muddle my way through all the clues."

"THAT'S IT, BILLY!" I screamed out loud, startling everyone so much that now they were on their feet. "You gave me a clue to look for."

"I did?" asked Billy. "*Ummm*, yeah, of course I did!" he echoed out loud.

"The clue in what he said was muddled," Dash barked to the others. "The grass was full of dew this morning when Max's dad came out to get the newspaper. I remember him taking his shoes off and commenting to me how wet the grass was just before he fed me. That means that whoever dug up the flowers would have had wet paws."

"Wet paws," I continued, "would lead to muddy paws. Paws that are muddy would have left a trail from the torn up garden to where they live! Let's see if there are any muddy paw prints anywhere around Doc's house."

Our feet hardly hit the ground as we tore around the Odell's house, a couple of times to make sure that we did not miss anything. Doc's wife, Mel, was a neat freak. She could not stand any dirt being on her white-tiled kitchen floor. If Annie was the culprit responsible for digging up the flowers, then she would have been yelled at this morning when she was let back inside. As we were circling the house, Doc came out on the back porch and asked what we were doing with such energy so early on a Sunday morning.

"We have to get back to rehearsals for the Fourth of July parade on Wednesday, Doc," I explained calmly, "But my mom told us we can't play with Annie outside of your yard unless you are around because she thinks Annie dug up her flowers."

"*Hmmm*, that sounds like a good reason not to let Annie out of the yard. If I know my dogs well, I would think Hera will stick by her side and not come out either. I don't think Annie was the culprit of this flower caper, but I can't tell for sure. Let me know if you boys need any help with your case," Doc noted. "I will be happy to help solve the mystery."

"We have only one question, Doc," Billy said. "Was Mrs. Odell angry this morning about how the kitchen floor looked?"

"No, sir, Mr. Rhu," Doc answered confidently. "I can honestly say that Mrs. Odell was not mad about anything. I sure hope that helps you solve this so Annie and Hera can be freed from their prison." With that answer, Doc closed the door and went back inside.

"That's it!" Billy exclaimed. "Open up the gate and let our parade cast out of the yard."

"Not so fast, Billy," Dash said and I translated. "In order to make sure that Annie is cleared from all wrongdoing and allowed back out with us, we not only have to prove she did not do it, but we have to find out who *did* do it."

"That might be the harder of the two," I said earnestly. "Who would have done such a thing?"

As the day progressed and the sun made its way across the cloudless blue sky, we kept having to move our setup to stay in the shade. Seconds ticked away into minutes, and minutes into hours. Before any of us knew it, Maggie and Grace were back, prodding us inside for lunch. "You told us that you would be ready for rehearsal after lunch, didn't you?" asked Maggie.

"Yeah," I replied, "but the mystery of who dug up Mom's flowers is taking longer than we expected. No one wants to start practicing more than me, but I just don't want to start without everyone there."

"You are going to have to face reality soon, Max," Dash quipped. "Annie and Hera might be locked in the yard for the rest of the summer."

"Maybe you need to practice without us," Annie said with her head pointed down and her tail still. "If Hera wants to go with you, I understand. But me, I'm stuck."

"There's no way I'm going to leave you in here alone," Hera told Annie, just a few feet away. "Never. All for one and one for all."

"Why is it every time we start to talk, these flea hotels start barking like crazy?" questioned Maggie. "I swear they are talking about us." As soon as Maggie finished that sentence, all four dogs barked and howled at once as if to respond to Maggie's statement.

"If she only knew," Dash said out loud.

"If only!" chimed in Waldo.

"Here is what I suggest," I said, trying to appease everyone involved. "We practice tonight after supper with whoever is present. If Hera and Annie are out by then, great. We can start with a full crew. If they are still stuck inside, not the best scenario but not the worst either. Can everyone agree with that?" I asked, almost scared to hear the answers.

"Sure," Maggie said on behalf of the high schooler contingent.

"Agreed," Billy said, speaking for the soon-to-be fifth graders.

"Well, do the dogs agree to this plan?" Grace said jokingly.

"We will be here!" woofed Dash, startling Grace who was in no way expecting a response.

"Supper is at five, so let's plan on 5:45 p.m. to start. Whoever is here is here," Maggie confidently said.

And with that, the four of us shook hands. On their way back inside, both girls patted all the dogs on their heads as if to admit the dogs were just as important to our parade success as they were.

CHAPTER 20

Time was running out. Not only on solving the mystery that was in front of us, but also before the parade was to start. We were less than three days away. We had not even attempted to pull the float with the girls.

As if he was reading my mind, Billy asked, "What if the girls can't pull the float? Then what? I have to be in the boat leading the way. I'm not sure this is going to work."

"Don't be such a Negative Nellie, Billy," I said. "I have a feeling things will work out. But let's solve one thing at a time. We definitely will not be able to get anything done without Hera and Annie. Let's make a list of all the facts and clues we have so far."

With this we wrote down everything we could: dew was on the grass this morning, no muddy paw prints into the Odell's house, no muddy paw prints leading up to the Odell's house, must have happened between midnight and 5:00 a.m., and not a raccoon or a possum. Over the next hour or so, we tried to go through every possible scenario out loud. Could Annie have done it and not remembered? No muddy paw prints inside. Could Hera have done it and not remembered? Again, no muddy paw prints. Dash was inside with Max. Waldo was inside with Billy. How could we figure this out?

"I got it!" exclaimed Dash. "We are fairly certain that the grass was wet this morning with dew. We can put that in the fact column. Since Max's dad had to put shoes on to go the paper, it was probably chilly and wet outside. Based on those facts, we can figure that whoever did dig up the flowers had cold, wet, and muddy paws," I said to Billy after Dash was done.

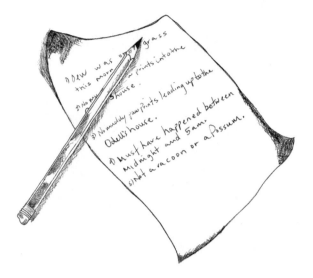

"And if the culprit did have muddy paws, then they had to have left a trail," I exclaimed out loud as if I had just found a pot of gold. "There should be a paw print trail right to the flower digger's house." Everyone was excited, jumping up and down and wagging their tails. Everyone, that is, except Annie.

"I don't want to get my hopes up, Max," bemoaned Annie. "I just don't want to get all excited about being able to play with my friends and have it not happen. I will be right here when you come back."

"Annie, we will do whatever we have to do to make sure that you can walk in the parade with us," I told her, scratching underneath her chin. "Let's go find us a flower digger!"

We all ran around to the front of our house. Billy and Waldo took one side of the front walkway while Dash and I took the other. We looked up and down the grass and the walkway, finding no paw prints. By this time in the day, all of the morning dew had dried off. We were back to square one, it seemed. We were all lying down on the grass in the front of our house, staring up at the blue sky and the few clouds overhead.

"I think that one looks like an orange," Billy said.

"An orange? Why not a baseball?" I quipped. "I mean, a circle is a circle."

"Yeah, I guess it could be a baseball, but I see an orange," Billy said, holding true to his first statement. "That one over there, that one reminds me of the state of Michigan. See there, it looks just like a mitten, just like Michigan," Billy went on.

Dash and I must have had the same idea at the exact same time together. "A mitten?" I inquired with him.

"Yes, a mitten. Like the kind you wear on your hands in the winter when you are young," Billy said to me very confidently.

"Billy, I think you just solved the case of who dug up the flowers," Dash exclaimed.

"You are a genius!" I translated from Dash to Billy. I was up on my feet, trying to pull Billy up so that we could confirm my latest notion.

"Can you explain to me how I just solved this mystery?" Billy said, still very perplexed as to what he had said or done to receive such high praise.

"It's simple, Billy. There are only a few people in this area that are up between midnight and five in the morning, the time frame that we are relatively sure the flowers were dug up. That number grows even smaller on the weekend, especially Sunday. There are not very many jobs that require folks to be at work that early every day of the week," I explained to Billy and Waldo. "But there are some jobs that require those who have them to work every day, Sundays, and even holidays. Everyone thinks about the usual—doctors, nurses, police officers, firefighters, and even doughnut makers. But everyone forgets about garbage men."

With that single word, Billy's face lit up with a smile. "Yeah, garbage men!" Billy said, turning his body to look at the house two doors down from our house. "That makes sense now."

"If we walk down to that house, I'm willing to bet that we see dirty paw prints on the walkway and stairs leading into the house. But we will have to be careful and quiet. Harold probably has not gotten home from work yet, and I do not want to upset his dog," I said, trying to sound as confident as I could because in reality, my stomach was shaking. I was so nervous.

The four of us walked across the grass and when we came upon the concrete walkway leading up to the house. "Get out of here! Who told you that you could walk on this grass or near this house! Scram! If I come out there, you will regret every move you ever made!" came a voice from behind the locked door. We started to turn to run away when Harold came out from behind the gate in the yard. "Max, come on over here please," Harold said in his typical soft tone of voice. "Is your mom home? If not, is your dad home? I have to apologize to them for what happened this morning. Arlo got out of the yard this morning when I was letting him out and putting on my work boots. By the time I was able to get my boots on and hunt him down, he had already dug all of your mom's prized flowers up out of the bed. I put him back on his leash and made sure the gate was locked and secured better. I am very sorry if you ended up taking part or all of the blame. I am not sure what happened or how he managed to get out, but I promise you the lock will always be secure. Ever since that time when you were younger and Arlo stole your mitten, I know I have to keep a very close eye on him. I wish he would not be so loud and rough. I would like to think he would have fun with you, Billy, and all of the other dogs on the block. Let me go inside and take these smelly clothes off. I will be right down to apologize to your parents and see how much money I owe them. Has the judging for the Fourth of July been completed yet?" Harold asked inquisitively.

"Luckily, the gardens were all judged yesterday, Mr. Dawgstnd. Otherwise, Arlo would have been in more trouble that I can imagine," I said very honestly.

"Well, I will be right down, Max. Please go tell your parents I'm on my way," Harold said as he ducked into his backyard. "And sorry if this has caused anyone any stress, but I did not think your parents would have wanted me ringing the doorbell so early."

I looked over at Billy, Waldo, and Dash who were all standing in a straight line. The tails were wagging in full windmill circles. "I think that just about wraps this case up, eh, Max?" Waldo quipped.

"This is over," I commented in a way that I hoped would answer Waldo and talk to Billy. "I think the only thing we have to do now is go tell Doc, Hera, and, of course, Annie. It will feel good to have the whole ensemble in place for our early evening parade rehearsal."

Harold was able to explain the situation to both my parents, Billy's dad, and the Odells all at once. My mom declined his offer to pay for any flowers that Arlo destroyed. She admitted she was thinking about redoing the front garden this fall anyhow. We sat and listened to what the adult were talking about for a few moments, but as soon as we were sufficiently bored, we crossed the street safely and went to our float. With such little time left, we really had to stay focused.

CHAPTER 21

Mr. Dawgstnd insisted that he pay for the damage Arlo had caused. My mom insisted that he not pay for the damage as she kept admitting that she was planning on digging up the entire garden this fall after school resumed. It was apparent that neither side was going to give in, so a compromise was reached.

"What if we all have a late afternoon grill out supper in your backyard?" Mr. Dawgstnd suggested. "That way, we can all talk and visit the Odells as well. If we have it in your backyard, Max and Billy's dogs will be able to attend."

"It can be the best of all worlds!" Grace exclaimed out loud, not really knowing how mean Arlo actually was.

"I don't think we need to include Arlo for this cookout," Mr. Dawgstnd replied. "He is not the friendliest of dogs right off the bat. Once he gets to know everyone, he is sweet as a kitten, but initially, he can be a little gruff."

I looked over at Billy who had a big grin on his face from ear to ear. "Max, this is going to be so fun. Maybe we can get Maggie and Grace to play us in a game of whiffle ball!" Billy said loudly, hoping that either Maggie or Grace would hear and agree. "We have not been able to play at all this summer since we've been so busy with the parade."

"I'm not so sure, Billy," I replied hesitantly. "I think we really need to at least make sure that all of the costumes fit well and there are not going to be any last-minute surprises or issues. We are not even a hundred percent sure this will work," I said sheepishly. "We have not practiced anything, with everyone in the right spots."

"Don't worry about it, Limburger breath," Maggie said from behind while starting to give me a noogie. Grace and I were doing some thinking and if you and Billy are up front on your bicycles pulling, each with one of the big dogs pulling next to you, we should have no problems."

"Yeah," echoed Grace. "We weigh almost nothing. Us two, plus the two little dogs standing as soldiers in the boat will be easy for such a strong pulling force. Max, I understand that you might be worried about it, so let's go practice the setup once or twice, quickly go over the costuming, and then we can come back for the cookout!"

I looked at Maggie and Grace, trying to figure out why they were being so nice. I was unable to see the angle in which they were working. "Why are you two wanting to help so much this afternoon?" I questioned. "When I think of Maggie and Grace, I normally don't think of cooperation."

"Listen, Max," answered Grace quietly, "we want to win just as badly as you do, if not more so. We don't care about the ribbons or the trophies, we just want to be, *umm*, well, *umm* . . ." Grace now hemmed and hawed.

"They just want to be with Teddy Huffnagle!" screamed Billy.

"Maggie and Teddy, sitting in a tree, k-i-s-s-i-n-g!" sang Dash and Waldo.

"STOP IT!" I hollered at once, looking in the direction of Billy, but really meaning it for the dogs. I reminded my buddy, "If we make fun of them too much, Billy, or make them uncomfortable about being in the parade with us, we are back to square one. We need them as much as they need us."

"*Ah*, I guess you're right, Max." Billy admitted. "I guess this is going to be the definition of cooperation. *Whelp*, let's head over to my garage and give the float a test pull."

As Maggie and Grace went upstairs to get the costumes that they had been working on, Billy and I gave our fathers a brief rundown of the pre-supper plan.

"Try not to work the girls too hard, boys," Billy's dad suggested. "If you make it miserable for them during rehearsals, they may want to up and quit. Girls can be a finicky group." He was now getting a very peculiar look from my mom. "You need to treat girls differently than you do the boys on your baseball team. You need to make them feel welcome. Otherwise . . . well, otherwise you might end up dancing by yourself in the corner while everyone else is dancing," Mr. Rhu said, getting a chuckle from my mom.

"Does anyone understand what he just said?" questioned Dash. "I'm really confused as to why dealing with girls is so much more difficult. We are around Hera and Annie all the time, and they are girls. They are never any problems."

I really did not know how to answer Dash, quite honestly. I have learned that Maggie is very set in her ways, and there are some things I just don't want to fight with her about. I just give in to her knowing that if I do get into a fight and Mom has to be involved, it's not going to end well for anyone. Just as I was trying to explain this to Billy, within earshot of the dogs, Maggie and Grace came out of the back door.

"You two look amazing!" chirped my mom. "You look so much better than I could have ever imagined."

I must admit, they did look really good. They had made Revolutionary War-style coats out of a couple of old coats my mom had up in a trunk in the attic. They glued colored pieces of felt on the pirate hats we got at Disney World many years back. What made the entire outfit was the white yarn that they wore as wigs.

"*Wow!*" I hollered with sheer delight. "You two look fabulous! Thank you both so much," I said without even thinking about it. I ran over to both Maggie and Grace and gave them a big hug. "We are going to win for sure."

The eight of us half walked, half hopped down the driveway to the curb where we all stopped. Although we were with older people, it was always our habit to stop and look both ways before we crossed. We even made the dogs sit at the curb to make sure we all crossed safely. Once we were across though, it was a sprint to the garage to open the door. The parade float was pulled out, the bicycles were attached, and lastly, the dogs' harnesses were laid out to get the most pulling power with the least amount of effort.

CHAPTER 22

"**W**hy was it decided that Maggie and Grace would be on the float?" asked Annie. "They were not part of the original idea. At first they said no. And they are just not very nice." She was a bit of annoyed in her query.

"We need them to make this work," I explained. "If we want to this float idea to succeed, then we have to include some other kids, and they are just as good as anyone." This statement immediately garnered a look of surprise from Maggie, Grace, and Billy.

"Them?" quipped Grace.

"We are more important to your parade float than just any two people from this town," Maggie said in the most defensive tone I had ever heard her use before. "We are more than just anyone, we are high school sophomores. With that comes an entire year of American history under our belts. We know all about Washington and his efforts. And with knowledge comes—"

"Power," interrupted Dash, looking smugly in my direction as he interrupted Maggie.

"Where would you have come up with such an idea," I directly asked Dash, knowing that all the other humans would wonder why I asked that and be looking straight at Dash.

"From Mrs. Murphy's history class," Grace tacked one. "Are you not paying any attention to what is being said around you, Max? It seems like all you are focused on is the dogs. Dogs, dogs, dogs. Can we just move on to the practice so we can wrap this up and start dinner? I'm starving."

Since it was starting to look like I was super focused on the dogs, I figured I better lay well enough alone and try to keep my attention on my parade partners and the float. When I had the chance to whisper to Dash, I took it. "We need to make sure no one is looking when I talk to you. There have been a few times today that I could have been caught."

"I know," said Dash. "You have to try and be more discreet. Can you imagine if anyone would find out about your talent?"

"Max!" yelled Maggie, once again interrupting me and Dash. "Can you come over here and bring one of the dogs to get them into the harness?"

I brought Dash over and put him in the harness closest to Billy's bike. Dash was the largest of the four dogs and understood me the best. I figured that he could help Billy pull on that side. If I needed him to step up the power, he could hear me the best. "Hera will go next to me," I said with a smile. Hera was an Alaskan husky, a sled dog. She had participated in very long dog races across Alaska, Canada, and Europe when she was younger. I knew she had the pulling notion down to a science.

"What about Waldo and Annie?" Billy asked. "Where will they go? We can't just have them with no leash on. They might get a ticket from Mr. Glenn Johnson, the dog catcher."

"Why not have them on the side of the boat on the float?" Maggie and Grace chimed in all at once.

"Simple," Waldo said with my translating a few seconds behind. "It would look like we were walking on water!"

"*Aha!*" Grace noted. "Good thinking, Waldo." I looked at her in stunned silence.

"Waldo?" I finally asked, having nervously gained the courage to ask. "Why Waldo?"

"It sounded like he was answering me," Grace dryly explained. I asked a question and he barked. Simple!" she said jokingly with a smile.

I looked over at Dash and shrugged. We both knew that I would really have to be careful about how much I talked to the dogs around other people. The last thing I wanted was to get caught and have to explain how I could understand them.

By this time, Hera had been put into her harness off to my right and Billy was on his bicycle to my left with Dash to his left.

Annie and Waldo were put inside the rowboat to look like soldiers of General Washington. Maggie and Grace climbed up and were in position in the boat as well. We all knew that only one more thing had to be done, see if the float could be pulled.

"Three, two, one," Maggie counted down. "Let's go!" she yelled at Billy and me.

We both started to pedal our bicycles as fast and as hard as we could. I could hear Dash and Hera's nails scraping on the ground. I briefly looked over at Billy only to see him head down and eyes closed, pedaling as hard as he could. I put my head down and shut my eyes, hoping that it might be just the extra power we needed to move the float. I pedaled as hard as I could for what seemed like hours, until, I heard Maggie screaming at the top of her lungs, "STOP! STOP! STOP! Look at where you are, you two!"

I immediately coasted on my pedals and looked up. As soon as I looked up, I pushed backward on my brakes, faster and harder than I had been pedaling.

"The street!" Billy screamed.

I'm not sure if he was yelling out of fear of going into the street or pure excitement that we had pulled the float fully loaded all the way down the driveway. I looked over at Billy to see the biggest smile I think I had ever seen from him. I imagined that as he looked back at me, he was thinking the same. Once we were fully stopped and had safely stopped the float, we let the dogs out of the boat and helped the girls off the stage platform.

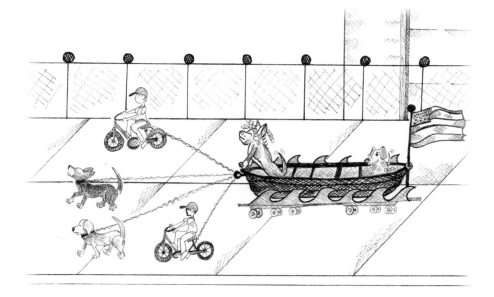

"That worked so well, Max!" Maggie said, somewhat surprised. "We are totally going to win on Wednesday. That went so smooth, I say we pull everything back up the driveway, put everything away, and head in for supper. I think I can smell the grill going now."

We all looked at one another in surprised disbelief that our plan actually worked. We worked together and cooperated. We slowly turned the float around and hopped back on our bicycles. Billy and I pedaled about half as hard as we did during the test run and still were able to easily pull it up the sloped driveway. Everything was put back into the garage and locked up. As a triumphant team, we walked back to our yard smiling with the anticipation of success. We sat around eating hot dogs, hamburgers, corn, and deviled egg potato salad. After supper, we ran around the yard trying to catch fireflies and playing hide-and- seek. It was a night to remember. There was no age difference between us. It did not matter that there was a big gap in school levels. It was just four kids and four dogs enjoying the warm summer night and basking in the glow of the rehearsal of our very own reenactment of one of the most famous scenes in American history.

A little after ten o'clock, my dad said, "It's about time you all get to bed. Tomorrow is Monday and then only be two more days until the parade. We still have to buy candy to toss on the parade watchers and tack up any dangling details." I was too tired to disagree. He was right, and I just wanted to crawl into bed.

"I will bring Dash in when I am done cleaning up," my mom said to me as she kissed my forehead when I walked by. "It looks like you just need to wash up and hit the sack."

I said goodnight to everyone present, slowly made my way upstairs, half-heartedly washed my face and brushed my teeth, and barely made it into bed before I fell asleep. I drifted off to dreamland thinking about the parade. I started to dream about being up on stage with Billy and the girls looking out at thousands of award ceremony attendees, all of them cheering my name. "Max! Max! Max! Max! Max! Max! Max!"

CHAPTER 23

"**M**ax! Max! Max!" I woke up, gently rubbing my eyes open. "It's almost eight! You almost slept through breakfast." I was surprised to hear my mom waking me up.

"Where is Dash?" I asked. "He always wakes me up at seven. Come to think of it, I don't think he came in at all last night."

"After you have brushed your teeth, come downstairs for breakfast," my mom said quietly. "I'm sure your dad will be able to answer all of your questions. I need to go out on assignment today so try not to make his day too hard. Neither one of us got a whole lot of sleep last night. Love you!" She kissed me on the head and was gone.

I quickly got up and went into the bathroom. After brushing my teeth and running a comb quickly through my hair, I bolted down the stairs. I looked into the kitchen to see my dad, Maggie, and Benji already up and seated at the table. No one was talking. "What's going on?" I asked. "And what is that horrendous smell?"

"Sir Fleabags decided that he wanted to ignore everyone calling his name last night and went out to protect us all from a skunk," Maggie told me, barely able to control her giggling. "He was sprayed at least twice."

"What? How does this happen? What does this mean? Dad?" I asked, feeling the tears welling up in my eyes. "W-what's next? Where is Dash? What happens?" I was asking questions as fast as my brain was able to process them. "Is he all right? Where is he?"

"Dash is OK, son," my dad said calmly, although to me looked like he was just dragged through a marathon. "Dash will be spending the next few days or even the next week outside in the yard. He got hit with skunk spray really bad. You can go visit him after you eat but you can't touch him. Don't worry, he is fine, and the smell will eventually wear off."

"Eventually?" I asked, trying to fight back the tears that had already started to roll down my cheeks. *Eventually.* The word rolled around my head like a single quarter in a soup can. How am I going to survive without my buddy next to me? How am I going to get any sleep knowing he is outside in the wild? Who is going to wake me up? My mind raced from one unanswered question to the next. "Dad, can I go see him? I'm not very hungry all of a sudden. I just really want to go see my best friend," I said, knowing my voice was shaking and tears were now hitting the table.

"Yes," answered Dad. "If you get hungry later, just come inside. But, Max, Dash is not allowed in the house."

"Yes, Dad," I replied. I knew that Dash was not going back in the house anytime soon, but it hurt to hear it said out loud.

As I opened the kitchen door to the yard, I saw Hera and Annie sitting on their side of the fence way in the back and staring at Dash who was sitting outside his doghouse. When we first got Dash, someone also gave us a doghouse that looks just like Snoopy's. Dash will occasionally go inside it if we are all out in the yard for some time. He goes in mostly for shade.

"Max!" Annie yelped. "Did you hear about Dash?"

"Of course he did, Annie," Hera scolded her. "Dash is always with Max. I'm guessing as soon as he woke up without Dash there, Max had to know."

Their little squabble usually made me laugh, but today, I was not even smiling a little. I made my way about halfway through the yard when—*Wham!* The stench hit my nose. "Holy buckets!" I screamed. "What is that?"

"*This* is what a skunk spray smells like," Dash said, peeking his head out of his house. "Last night when the adults were cleaning up, I saw two beady eyes behind my house. I thought it was a cat so I took off yelling, 'Scram! Scram! Scram!' But as soon as I got close enough to realize it was a skunk, I saw the tail curl up from behind and *kapow!* I was hit. It sprayed me so much my eyes were burning and watering. Doc Odell came running right away and scared the skunk off. Your dad and Doc then put me immediately into the kid's pool, hosing me off. That did nothing for the smell. Then they tried tomato juice. Nothing."

"Tomato juice?" I interrupted. "You got sprayed by a skunk, not run over by a ravioli cart!" I quipped, making myself and Annie laugh.

"Supposedly, tomato juice binds to the stink molecules then you would be able to rinse the stench off. But as you can tell, it does not work," Dash went on. "They washed me a couple of more times throughout the night with all things Doc had down at his office. Some of the things were able to cover up the smell for a short while but none of them worked for very long. I'm sorry, Max."

"Sorry about what, Dash?" I asked him, feeling horrible for my buddy. "You did not cause this!"

"I overheard your mom and dad talking about the parade. They said that there was no way they could let me be in the parade smelling like this. I will have to stay home."

I was so worried about Dash that I totally forgot about the parade. I had not thought about anything else for a couple of weeks now, and with Dash stuck in the doghouse, I forgot about it.

"What are we going to do, Max?" Annie asked quietly as if not to upset anyone more than they were. "Now what? Do we need to start looking for another dog to help out? I have some friends at the dog park that are yappy and full of energy. They could help."

"All of our dog park friends are too small, Annie," Hera snapped back. "They are all little dogs. Dash was one of the main dogs pulling up front with me. Maybe Waldo can stand in for him."

"I don't think so, Hera," Dash said. "Waldo is scrappy but his paws are sensitive. He can't walk for a long time on the hot asphalt."

As their discussion kept going, I was thinking about all of the hard work we had put into the parade float. *Maybe it would be best if we just decorated our bikes individually*, I finally thought. *This idea is doomed.*

CHAPTER 24

"**M**ax!" screamed Billy, standing at the sidewalk in front of our house. "Max! Can you come down here so I can talk to you?"

"Come on back!" I yelled right back at him. "I'm here with Dash in the doghouse."

"I know!" Billy responded. "My dad told me I'm not to go anywhere near Dash today. I have to go see my doctor later so he doesn't want me to stink like skunk. I won't be able to do anything today. We can practice for the parade first thing in the morning. See you later!" With that, I lost my two best friends for the day.

By the time lunch came around, I became accustomed to how Dash smelled. Dash was lying on his back just in front of his house. Hera was in the shade of the large maple tree in the Odell's yard. Annie was on the scorching hot concrete patio behind their house. Dad and Benji brought out a ham sandwich and lemonade for me, a bowl of kibble for Dash, and a few slices of bacon to share.

"Don't tell Mom I made these for you two," Dad whispered even though Mom was away on assignment. "I can tell you two are having a bad day."

"Thanks, Dad," I replied, truly thankful. "Is there anything we can do to get the stink off Dash? I don't want him to stink during the parade on Wednesday."

"Well, buddy," my Dad said, switching his stare back and forth from Dash to me, "Mom and I agree that if Dashman stills smells like a skunk on Wednesday, he won't be able to go to the parade. We know how much you have worked on it with Billy and even the girls, but we just can't. We don't want to ruin anyone else's day by having Dash stinking all over town. I'm sorry."

I could feel the tears rolling down my cheeks. I knew he was right but again, it just hurt to hear it out loud. All of a sudden, I heard Doc's gate open and felt the sudden burst of Annie running like the wind. As I braced myself for being tackled over, all I felt was her soft tongue licking the dripping tears away. I looked up to see both my Dad and Doc.

"Max, after supper tonight, we can try and wash Dash a few times using all of the at home shampoos that we have at the veterinary office," Doc said in his own style. "I know how much you love Dash and all the dogs so this experiment will be on me. I can tell my clients that all of them were Dash tested and Max approved." Annie had just stopped licking my tears away when he finished. I hopped up and hugged Doc, thanking him for trying to help.

"We will be ready for the washing by 7:00 p.m., Doc," my dad said loud enough for Doc to hear as he was walking toward his car. "You must be a pretty special duo if everyone is trying to help you two out. Be thankful that you are surrounded by so many people who care," Dad said to me, looking at Dash.

As the rest of the afternoon progressed, nothing much changed. I napped with my head resting on Dash. Hera slowly moved every once in a while to stay under the shade as the sun slowly began to set. Annie flipped herself over every now and again, making sure to only bake each side of her body for so long in the sun. I sprinted inside exactly at five for supper. I was out immediately after doing my chores of washing the dishes and taking out the garbage. I paced up and down the fence line, not so patiently waiting for Doc to come out. Finally, with two minutes to spare, Doc came out of his back door with a few bottles of dog shampoo.

"One of these has to work, Max," Doc stated loudly. "Or if just one does not, maybe all of them together will!"

"I sure hope so," Hera said, now facing the other direction. "That dog smells."

CHAPTER
25

Doc Odell walked through the gate and motioned for me to bring Dash over by the pool. "We need to follow the directions properly," Doc told me and Dash. "Where is everyone?"

"Well, Billy had to go to the doctor, Mom is still on assignment, and Dad says that he can't be out here close to Dash," I said nervously. "You will be able to save Dash, won't you, Doc? I will get my buddy back?" I asked, feeling the tears start to well up again.

"I will do my best, Max," Doc stated plainly. "I'm not sure how long it will take for the stink to totally wear off but it will eventually. I heard through grapevine that you need Dash for your Fourth of July parade entry. I think we need to work our hardest to get him back to tip-top shape."

The plan was simple. I hold Dash while standing in the pool. Doc runs the hose and pours whatever product we are using for that round, I work it in and scrub it through Dash's fur, and then Doc rinses the stuff out. Then we give Dash the smell test. First, we went with the tomato soup.

"Why tomato soup, Doc?" I asked. "Why not something else, like cream of mushroom or chicken noodle? Chicken noodle smells a whole lot better than yucky tomato."

"The acidic nature of the tomatoes binds to the molecules of the skunk spray, covering them in a layer of anti-stink of sorts. It does not actually remove the smell, Max, but only masks the smell," Doc explained. "The other ones we are going to try will actually work on breaking the bond between skunk and fur."

As Doc starting spraying Dash, he whined, "This is so humiliating. I'm going to look like a wet rat."

After the tomato soup was worked into Dash's fur then rinsed out, I gave him a good hard, long whiff with my nose. "Nope," I sighed, "Yuck!"

Over the next hour and a half, Doc and I tried multiple de-skunk smell products. Hera, Annie, and even Waldo made their way into the backyard to lie around in the grass and commentate on the proceedings.

"How could you let a skunk get that close to you, in your own yard even," joked Waldo. "I would have snuck up from behind and flung him by his tail."

"I would have just barked and yelled until he was so scared of me that he would have run away," Annie snickered.

Hera stayed oddly silent, except to say in her best Batman impression, "Still stinky!" after each product we tried on Dash.

"Well, Max," quipped Doc, "we have only one more of the miracle cures left. This one says to apply to a dog whose fur is damp, not wet. We will work the goop into Dash's fur and then leave it on overnight. Maybe you and your dad can rinse Dash in the morning to see if we were successful."

"Of course, Doc, whatever you recommend," I answered him back. "I want to get Dash back up to full speed as soon as possible!"

With that, Doc let the anti-stink stuff run all over Dash's head, back, and legs. I rubbed and worked it in all over his body until he was covered in a very light foam. As we let the product set, it started to actually smell nice.

"*Hey!*" said Waldo, trying to remain cheerful for Dash. "This stuff seems like it might just work."

"I sure hope I never have to go through such a humiliating experience," Annie said confidently. "But again, there's no way I would ever be caught so close to a skunk."

As we cleaned up the yard and put everything away, Dash slowly made his way back to his doghouse for the night. Doc walked back through his gate and called for Hera and Annie. "Bye-bye," Doc said in his trademark goodbye.

Annie sprinted all the way from the back corner of our yard straight into her's. Hera got up from the comfortable spot that she made next to Dash's doghouse and said politely, "Still stinky."

"Thanks, Hera. You really know how to cheer a guy up," Dash said as she slowly walked toward the gate and then into her house.

"I don't want to get anyone's hopes up, Dash. We have all seen how much Max and Billy have worked on the parade float. I just think . . . well, I just think we need to be realistic about this. I think Max and Billy need to spend tomorrow decorating their bicycles," Hera said just prior to going through the kitchen door.

"What do you think, Dash?" I asked my best buddy. "What do you think we should do? I don't want to leave you at home, but I also know what Billy is hoping for. If you can't help us pull the float in the parade, then we can't even start. If that is the case, then, yeah, I think we need to work on our bikes tomorrow."

"In that case," Dash said, turning away from me as he said it, "wake up early tomorrow and decorate your bikes after breakfast. We can rinse this stuff out of my fur later after lunch. None of this stuff has worked so far. Just like Hera said, still stinky."

Dash crawled to the very back of his doghouse and curled up into his ball to fall asleep. I tried to reach my hand in to rub his head but all I was able to touch was a still tail. Not even a little bit of a wag. I got up, slowly walked inside, and went upstairs to wash my face and brush my teeth. When I got into bed, I scraped my foot on Dash's favorite chew toy. I realized that there was nothing that could be done to fix this. I fell asleep with tears of failure soaking into my pillowcase.

CHAPTER 26

I woke up the next morning alone and by myself. No one woke me up. When I looked at the clock, it was almost nine. I hurried up and got ready for the day, knowing that it was not going to be what I had hoped for the day before the parade. I made my way downstairs and into the kitchen where Maggie and Grace were already eating at the table.

"Are we ready for a big win tomorrow?" Grace asked, smiling from ear to ear. "Are we ready to be awarded all of the prizes in the parade? *Ah*, come on Max, we are a shoo-in for some type of win!"

"What's the matter, Max?" asked Maggie, as if she didn't know. "So what if Dash has to be left at home. There was enough pull power during our test run to make this work just fine. If we back out now . . . well, I don't know what will happen. But I do know we won't win."

"I think I'm going to tell Billy to decorate his bicycle for the parade. I just wanted him to get something for himself. I wanted Billy to feel like a winner this year. I-I just wanted him to feel happy and like a winner. That was all messed up the other night when Dash was just trying to protect the family."

I looked up to see my dad staring at me. When we made eye contact, he tilted his toward the back door and the yard. I took that to mean that I was allowed to go see Dash. I slowly made my way out of the kitchen and into the yard. As usual, Annie was basking in the sun on the concrete and Hera was sprawled out in the shade adjacent to Dash's doghouse. As I walked toward his house, Hera looked at me and said, "Still stinky." I knew any chance of our float entering the parade was now gone.

When I got to Dash's house, I saw that his bowl still had most of the kibble in it from this morning. "Dad came out, gave me my breakfast early, and then went right back inside. I did not even get the chance to come out and have him pet me," Dash explained from way back in his house. "Hera's right, I'm still stinky."

"I just don't know what to say, Dash," I explained to my pal. "I just don't know what to say to anyone. I know you feel horrible about being stinky, but I also know Billy feels horrible a lot of the time because his mom died. I was just trying to make my friend feel better." I think my head was as low as Dash's.

"Then go over to his house with your sister and Grace and practice. You have an extra bike in the garage. Take that one over and decorate it with Billy. If you can't pull the float, then at least he will have something to enter," Dash explained, head still facing the back of the doghouse.

"Are you sure, Dash?" I asked, not knowing if this was the best idea or just him trying to make me feel better.

"I'm sure," Dash replied. "When you are all done with his stuff, you can come back over and rinse this goop off me. I will still be here."

I took Dash's word that he wanted me to go practice with Billy. I walked back up to the house, opened the door, and asked the girls if they were ready to practice. We all walked across the street to Billy's who was outside in the yard with Waldo. I explained to him what my plan was. He slowly agreed after asking at least ten times if this is was I really wanted. We then went back to my garage, got my old bicycle so he could decorate it, and let Hera and Annie out to come over and practice. The girls got up on the platform as Billy and I placed Waldo into Dash's harness. Billy put special dog booties on Waldo's paws to protect them from the heat of the concrete and asphalt. With everyone in place, Maggie yelled, "Go!"

Billy and I started to pedal as fast and as hard as we could. Although it was not as easy as it was with Dash up front, the four of us were able to pull the girls and Annie in the on the parade float attached to four skateboards. We slowly made the turn onto the sidewalk and for the next three hours, pulled the float up and down the block. I was excited to see that our idea was going to work for the parade and for Billy, but I was also sad because my best buddy in the whole world was not going to be able to be there with us. After everyone decided that we were set for the next day, we went across the street back to our house for lunch.

"How goes the big parade float, gang?" my dad asked as the four of us descended into the kitchen for lunch. "It looked like you were able to swap out Waldo for Dash without any real issues. I know it is not the first plan, but good for you all for being able to switch things up and still enter. Cooperation and versatility at its best."

As Maggie, Grace, and Billy made their own sandwiches, I quickly made mine and snuck out the door to go see Dash. When I made it back to his house, the front half of his body was outside the door. He was lying flat with his snout on his front paws. "I don't think this stuff is going to work, Max," Dash quietly said. "But at least it looked like I was not missed during rehearsals."

"Of course you were missed, Dash," I said honestly. "You were one of the main motivators that made us want to try this. You are part of the team. I'm going to ask Dad that if you are not *too* stinky tomorrow, he could bring you so to watch the parade." Dash slowly looked up at me and then retreated back into his doghouse. I looked over and saw both Hera and Annie just on the other side of the fence. "Do you think you two can come over and cheer him up just a bit?" I asked.

"We can at least try," Hera replied. This was the first time I heard Hera talk in her own voice and not her Batman impression in a few days.

I hurried over and opened the gate, allowing Hera and Annie to run over and lay next to Dash's house. Soon after, Billy and the girls came out and asked if I wanted to go to the community pool to go swimming. "Tammi just got hired as the new lifeguard," Maggie explained. "She told us that she would use her free passes on us!"

"No, thank you, but take Billy if he wants to go please," I asked Maggie, gently nudging her to take my friend so I would be able to have some alone time with the dogs. It was evident that Billy wanted to go as he sprinted across to his house and brought back his bathing suit, towel, goggles, and Waldo. He led Waldo into our yard where he trotted back to the crowd at Dash's doghouse, only to turn around and see our three teammates head off for the pool. I spent the rest of the afternoon in the shade with Hera, watching Waldo and Annie position themselves for the maximum amount of sun-baking time. Dash remained in his doghouse, all curled up.

Doc came over to the yard just after supper that night. I explained that I did not want to attempt to rinse Dash off without Doc being present and make the situation worse. "I understand, Max," Doc said easily. "Let's get the hose out and see how well it worked."

I coaxed Dash out of his house and into the pool. Doc held the hose high as we rinsed Dash off, creating a horrible puddle of grayish brown water in the bottom of the pool. "At least it got all of the dog cooties off of him," Annie snapped while sniffing the rinse water. "Yuck!"

Hera walked over and gave Dash a good long sniff after we had finished with the rinse. We all looked at her as if she was the judge of how Dash smelt. She lifted her snout up toward the sky as if to ask me to rub her neck before passing judgement on Dash. I quickly gave her chin and neck a quick scratch to get her ready to speak. Hera lowered her snout down, looked at Dash, then me, and then back at Dash. "Still stinky." Dash hopped out of the pool and made a beeline for his doghouse. I thought about going after him but I was not sure what to say or how to act.

"Doc, can you please make sure Waldo gets home tonight," I asked quietly. "Tomorrow is a big day and I want to get a good night's rest."

"Of course, Max," Doc said dryly. "Never a problem. Good night, Max. Bye-bye."

I walked up to the door and into the house. I went in; kissed my dad, mom, and Benji good night, and went upstairs and got ready for bed. As I laid in bed waiting to fall asleep, I resigned myself to the notion that tomorrow was the annual Fourth of July parade, Dash's first, and he was not even going to be able to attend. I fell asleep gently crying again.

CHAPTER
27

Both Mom and Dad came in just before seven to wake me up. "I'm sorry, buddy," Dad started out by saying, "but we just went outside and although Dash smells so much better than before, we both think that he does not smell good enough to take him with us for the parade."

"I know how much this hurts now, but at some point, you will understand," my mom said, doing her best to make me feel better. "You have no idea how proud we are of you, doing all of this and even being able to cooperate with your sister, all so that Billy can feel like a winner. It has been a very rough year for him. When we talked to his dad, his dad was proud that you are his friend. Just realize you are making a big difference in his life as well."

"I know, Mom," I quietly replied, "But I just wanted Dash to be there with us. This is Dash's first Fourth of July, and I wanted all of us to win together. Will he be able to come out with us tonight to watch the fireworks?"

"Of course, he can, Max. But just remember that not all dogs like fireworks so he may be scared," my dad quickly reminded me. "Remember Waldo last year? When we were gone, he ate all of the Whoppers candy!"

At that, even I laughed and got up to get ready. The parade started at noon but we had to check into the bicycle corral at ten. Before breakfast, I quickly ran outside to see Dash eating his kibble, outside his doghouse. "It sure looks like you are feeling better this morning," I said to Dash.

"I am," replied Dash, back at his normal voice level. "I'm feeling good. As soon as you all win first prize, I know you will come and get me for the rest of the events today. And Max, remember, no matter what, I will always be with you. You are trying to make your friend feel better. You are trying to cheer Billy up. I am proud of you because of that. We all are." He looked over the fence, seeing Hera and Annie staring at us. "Although you are a soon to be ten-year-old, you sure act much older than that. Be good, pedal steady, and bring back at least one blue ribbon!"

With that, the three dogs around me started barking as loud as they could. Doc came out of his house to see what all the commotion was. Dad opened up to door and started to laugh while calling me in for breakfast. "I am sure Dash is telling you to 'Win one for the Gipper'!" Dad yelled. "Come on in and eat up. You need your strength and we need to get ready to leave."

I looked Dash in his eyes, which were locked on mine, and rubbed just behind his ears. "Not only do I want to win for Billy, but I also want to win for you." With that, I turned around and quickly made my way into the house.

After breakfast was over, I cleaned up a little before nine. Maggie and Grace came down from her bedroom, wearing knee-high white socks, black patent leather schools shoes, dark green sweatpants rolled up to their knees, long coats, and the white wigs made from yarn. Billy came over looking splendid in a long-sleeved white shirt and blue shorts.

"You all look so marvelous!" Mom said, her voice cracking. "The best part is you are all working together and cooperating. Although you may be in it for different reasons—"

"Us for a ribbon, you for a boy," interrupted Billy, getting a laugh from my dad.

"Yes, Billy. You a ribbon, them a boy," my mom agreed, "But you are all working toward the same goal. We are all very proud of you."

"The float is too large to put in the car, Max, so you and Billy can start to ride it to the school parking lot when you are ready. I will bring Hera, Annie, and Waldo along with the girls in the car," my dad said. "Mom and Billy's Dad will bring our seats and stuff in just a bit. Be careful and try not to run anyone over on the sidewalks. If you have to, you may ride in the street but only to go around people." Billy and I looked at each other and sprinted off to his garage.

"Do we have everything?" Billy asked nervously. "I mean, do we have everything?"

"Slow down, Bill," I asked him. "All we need is the float, bicycles, and the two harnesses for Hera and Waldo. Annie will be leashed into the boat. Let's start riding and see how things go."

We got on our bikes and started to pedal. Without any weight on the float, it pulled smoothly. We gauged how much stopping power we needed early on so by the time we were at the school parking lot, we were experts.

"Max Booker and Billy Rhu checking in, sir," I said proudly to the grandfather who was standing at the parking lot entrance with the clipboard.

"What are you entering for?" he asked, rather inquisitively. "I am not sure we have a float division!"

"The bicycle parade division," I said, feeling my adrenaline start to take over. "There are no rules that say we can't enter with a float. Just as long as there is a bicycle involved, I think that we should be able to enter," I started to rattle off faster and faster. I could feel myself getting more and more upset.

"Slow down, Max," the man said to me. "I agree with you. The rules are set for everyone to enter no matter what. I was just giving you a bit of a hard time. It looks great! I can't wait to hear the description."

"Luckily, the girls took care of that last night, Max," Billy told me. "We forgot that we needed a bunch of words so that the judges can hear them when we are in front of the judges' station with Mayor Huffnagle watching." When Billy finished that sentence, Maggie, Grace, Hera, Annie, and Waldo all arrived.

"Things are looking great, guys!" my dad said excitedly to us. "It looks like there is going to be fine competition, but I do know you all have the finest float depicting Washington's crossing of the Delaware here."

"Delaware?" I asked. "Delaware? We thought all along it was the Potomac."

"Nope," Dad replied dryly. "I'm sure it is the Delaware. I don't think you have to worry about it at all. Just focus on a good steady pace and don't hit the brakes too hard as the float might crash into your bikes."

"I feel like we are doomed now, Billy," I tried to calmly tell him. "We have had the wrong event the entire time! It is destiny now that we are going to do badly. Why didn't the girls catch that? They were the ones who had American history in school. I mean, they only told us how many times." I could feel my adrenaline rising yet again. "Girls, why?" I said, turning around to ask them directly. "Wait, where are they?" I asked sharply. Billy pointed across the parking lot to where our George Washington and his first aide were sitting on the steps in front of Teddy Huffnagle who was wearing his baseball uniform. Both Billy and I just stared. "I hope they remember why we are all here," I said to Billy. "I don't know much about girls, but from what I hear coming from Maggie's room when they are alone, they would follow Teddy anywhere. I just hope that they don't leave us without a general."

"They won't, Max," Billy reassured me. "I think they have as much in this as we do. Plus, it is almost eleven o'clock and even your sister would not leave us this close to parade time."

I looked over at Billy and shrugged. I guess he was right. Even my sister would not be that mean. "Here they come now," I said out loud to anyone that might be listening. "One more quick review of the parade route and we will be ready for launch."

Maggie and Grace made their way back to our group. Maggie said while looking directly at me, "Max, Teddy's team is playing St. Ignatius over at that ball field. He asked if we could come watch. I know how much you and Billy worked on this but—"

"Go!" I said, not allowing her to even finish. "Go watch Teddy play. Billy and I will be fine."

As soon as I said this, Grace gave out a very loud, "*Wahoo!*"

"No!" my parents said in almost perfect unison. "You can't just bail out on your brother. Do you not realize how much this means to them? They have worked every day, almost since school let out, to make this a reality. You promised us that you would help them.

If you leave, I can guarantee you will be grounded for the rest of the summer."

Without even letting Maggie reply, I said, "Mom, it's OK. As much as we want to win, I'm sure that is how much they want to go see Teddy. Everyone should have the right to get what they want."

My mom's jaw had dropped open. Billy's dad's eyes were red. My dad was just shaking his head. "If that's what Max wants, then I guess go. But leave your wigs here," my dad dryly said. "I'm not very happy about this and we will talk about this later, but go ahead. Be home by dusk for the fireworks."

Maggie and Grace ripped out their wigs before he had finished. "Thank you so much, Max!" Maggie squealed as they hugged us both and ran off.

"I forgot something at home," my dad said. "I'll be right back. It is only a five-minute drive." He was gone.

Over the next thirty minutes, Billy and I got things ready. We decided that he would stand in the front of the rowboat with Annie in the back tied in. We rearranged the bicycles so that mine was in the middle with Hera and Waldo on each side. After having Billy crawl up and into the boat with Annie, I gave this setup a rehearsal pull.

"It won't be easy," I said after making a few laps around the parking lot, "but I will do my best to make it work. Any port in a storm is a saying I once heard." I looked up at the big clock on the wall of the school. We had less than fifteen minutes until the parade started.

"All bicycle parade participants, please line up according to your bib number," was announced over the bullhorn. "Please line up on the yellow parking stripes so we can start promptly at noon."

"Promptly at noon, promptly at noon," I heard in a parrot voice. "We can start promptly at noon." I spun around to see my dad had Dash on a leash.

"Dash!" I yelled as loud as I could. "Dash, you're here!"

"I am here," Dash said calmly and dryly. "I'm missing my early afternoon nap to be here. Your Dad came and got me, explaining on the way over how he has never, and most likely never will, be able to explain or understand girls. But here I am, so let's get all set up for a parade."

"Dash!" Billy yelled just about as loud as me. "You made it!"

"I know how much you boys worked on this all summer," Dad went on to explain. "I did not want anyone to have to smell Dash when we were sitting on the curb. But if he is *in* the parade, I don't think anyone will notice. With the girls gone, Mom will push Benji in his stroller and Billy's dad and I will walk behind tossing out the candy. Let's hurry up and get Billy's bike tied back on."

Luckily, we were the last entry in the parade. We hurried up to get everything as set as we could. "Who is going to be Washington?" my mom asked.

"Dash," Billy and I said at the same time. "He is best choice."

We loaded Annie up in the back where she promptly laid down on the rowboat bench seat. That was OK. As Dash walked by Hera, she said, "Not so much stinky," which at least made me laugh.

Dash was strapped into place. Hera and Waldo were rearranged up front with the addition of Billy's bicycle to help me pull. At five minutes past noon, we were off.

CHAPTER 28

The parade was perfect. Billy and I did not have to pedal nearly as hard as when the girls were on the float. My mom was able to make Grace's wig fit and stay on Annie's head with almost no problems. She used the inside cardboard from a few rolls of paper towels to create a powdered wig for Dash. Every so often, I would sneak a peek back to see what our float looked like, always seeing Dash standing up with his back paws on the bench seat and his front paws on the bow. It really looked like he was proudly standing just like Washington did in all of the pictures I had ever seen.

After the parade was over and all of the entrants gathered at the baseball field, people came up to Billy and me to congratulate us on our float. I don't think either of us had ever shaken so many hands before. Teddy's baseball game had just ended when Maggie and Grace were able to make their way back over to where we were sitting in the shade. Just as Maggie was going to ask how it went, Mayor Huffnagle got on the microphone.

"We would like to announce all of the winners in this year's Fourth of July parade. Before we continue, however, we would like to remind everyone that the fireworks will take place just after dusk near the town square. As in year's past, the display should be viewable from almost anywhere in town. With that business out of the way, let's award some prizes! If you hear you name, please come up on stage to receive your prize and stick around up here for the annual winner's photo." The first four prizes went by quickly. With only one more ribbon left on the table, my heart started to pound so hard I thought it might come right out of my chest. "And this year's winner for Most Patriotic is . . . Jimmy Riordan!" The crowd clapped so loud, I did not hear what my dad had said to me.

I was stunned. I looked over at Billy who was smiling ear to ear, clapping wildly. "Billy," I tried to speak but was drowned out by the crowd noise. "I'm so sorry. I really thought this idea was a winner."

"Don't worry about it, Max," he replied, still smiling and clapping. "Jim's bicycle looked amazing. No one will ever be able to forget him. Plus, look how much time we were able to spend together working on this. Look at how much fun we had. That is all I wanted anyways!"

I was not sure how to react. I wanted a victory. I wanted a blue ribbon. I stood there thinking about everything that we had been through. Maybe I wanted the victory more for me than for Billy. As I was lost in my thoughts, I was shaken by my dad to look up and follow Billy. As I looked up, I saw the entire town staring at me. Up on stage was Mayor Huffnagle looking directly at me and motioning for me to step up on stage.

"There is one last prize for this year's parade," Mayor Huffnagle announced to the crowd. "Although this has traditionally been a bicycle parade, this year we had an amazing entry. When I spoke with their fathers earlier this week, I was told at how much these two young men had worked on their float. They did this all on their own. These two young men were able to think about how to secure the stage to the wheels, how to secure the boat to the float, and, most importantly, figure out how to place the pulling power to make sure everyone here was able to see their depiction of Washington crossing the Delaware. Our top prize has always been Most Patriotic. This year, however, in accordance to be fair and on par with most entries of this kind, we will have an additional category that I think everyone will agree that Billy Rhu, Max T. Booker, and crew has won. Will everyone please clap their hands for the winners of . . . BEST IN SHOW!"

The entire assembled crowd clapped, hooted, and hollered even louder than for Most Patriotic. After Billy and I were given our blue ribbons, Hera, Annie, Waldo, and Dash were all given small blue ribbons to hang from their collars. We managed to get all four dogs looking at the camera for a couple of photos with the winners of the other categories. As we walked back to where our families were, people in the crowd patted us on the backs and told us what a fabulous job we had done. Even Mr. Sutherland, who was visiting from Scotland, told us that we had done a 'brill' job (I thought that was very sporting of him as his country was on the losing end of what General Washington was fighting for!). Both of our families hugged us and told us how proud of us they were. Maggie even hugged me. That never happens. I looked over and saw Billy and his dad hugging, both with tears streaming down their faces.

"I wish Mom was here to see this, Dad," Billy said quietly to his dad but just loud enough for me to make out.

"I do too, Bill," his dad said. "But we both know she is here in her own sorta way."

CHAPTER
29

We were not the only ones being congratulated that day. All the dogs in the neighborhood came up to my four canine friends and told them how proud everyone was. Even Arlo barked his thoughts that evening from inside his locked yard. Mom and Dad were right, Dash was not a huge fan of the fireworks so he was able to spend the fireworks display in the basement with Hera, Annie, and Waldo all there for comfort.

As everyone was cleaning up and heading for their own homes, Billy came over and shook my hand. "Congratulations, Max! And thanks," he said, looking right at me.

"No need to thank me. This is what best friends do," I replied, both turning our heads so the other would not see the tears beginning to form.

When we went inside, just before getting ready to go to sleep, I asked my mom if Dash was able to come inside tonight. "Not yet," she said. "He is still pretty stinky."

Dash and I immediately looked at each other in disbelief. "No, she can't understand us, can she?" Dash barked quietly.

"She is *my* mom, Dash, so you never know!" I replied.

"But if you want, you can take your sleeping bag and go out back and sleep next to his doghouse," my dad chimed in with from the living room.

I could not get up and down the stairs fast enough after having grabbed my pillow and bag. That was the first night that I slept outside with Dash near his doghouse but certainly not the last.

The next few weeks were uneventful. Nothing really happened until Billy and I were both assigned to Mrs. Bahador's fifth grade classroom. We were ecstatic that we had been placed in the same room. Later that week, we were told a new family was moving in. Mom and Dad told Maggie and me at supper one night that they would probably be invited over for a meet and greet soon after they moved in. To Maggie's delight, Mom told us that they had four children: Mary, who was Maggie's age, and triplets Jack, Sam, and Mack. They also had two dogs, greyhounds. As soon as supper had finished, I ran to the curb, stopped, looked both ways, and then sprinted as fast as I could to Billy's house hoping that he had heard the exciting news.

"Billy, we are going to be getting three new kids on our block. The best part is that they are our age and are boys!" I said, not sure if he understood anything I said.

"Not so fast there, Max!" Mr. Rhu said, folding down his newspaper and looking in from the living room. "Do you want to tell him or should I, Billy?"

"I guess he should hear it from me," Billy said. "Bad news always seems to be less harsh if you hear if from someone you are best friends with. Only part of what you said was correct."

"What?" I asked, knowing exactly what my parents had told me. "Our age, kids, three boys. What is not correct?"

"Those are sneaky names," Billy said to me as he led me to one of the kitchen chairs. "Their names—Jac, Sam, and Mac—are actually, Jacquelyn, Samantha, and Mackenzie. They are girls."

I felt like someone had just stepped on my chest. "Girls?" I asked. "Girls? But those are boy's names. Who would be so sneaky as to name their girls with boy's names?"

"Better get used to the idea, boys," Billy's Dad said with a hint of a chuckle in his voice. "Those dirty girls you two are always trying to avoid are going to become a big part of your lives very soon!" With that sentence, he did start to laugh.

I got up and slowly walked across the street. Dash was sitting in the backyard alone. "I already heard," he said. Hera and Annie told me all about them. They have four daughters and two dogs. Doc Odell says that they are very good-looking dogs. Let's not worry too much about them just yet, Max. Let's give them a try."

As the night wore on, Dash and I talked all about what had happened to us since he came to live at our house. We both threw our heads back and laughed about the first time I learned he could talk when both of us were running away from Arlo and how close I was to being caught more than once talking to him, Hera, Annie, and Waldo. We were now able to laugh uncontrollably at how bad he smelled after being sprayed by the skunk. We rolled around on the grass out by his doghouse. I scratched his neck, behind his ears, and, as he wiggled into position, a full-body rubdown. I smiled as he stretched out like Superman, back leg muscles bulging from his skin. He even smiled. I looked up into the sky and pointed out the North Star to him as he laid his head on my lap.

"Best friends forever?" he asked.

"Best friends forever."

ABOUT THE AUTHOR

Pat Moon has traveled the world; he is always on the lookout for his next big adventure, usually finding it in places most people can only dare dream about. No matter where his travels may take him, from the Alaskan tundra to the Highlands of Scotland, seeing India on a tuk-tuk to watching giraffes in Africa by bush plane, Pat is always happy to come home to Chicago. He lives there with his wife, three dogs, two cats, and a never-ending list of where to go next. He always seems to keep a smile on his face and his next journey in mind. Pat is endlessly excited to share his latest adventures with children, focusing on never letting go of a dream and conquering whatever hurdle might be in the way. Pat is constantly ready, willing, and able to take part in whatever crazy idea comes up next in his life!

CPSIA information can be obtained
at www.ICGtesting.com
Printed in the USA
FSHW010212011218
53935FS